DON'T

LOOK

INSIDE

SPIKE BLACK

Published by High Concept Books

ISBN-10: 1492227757
ISBN-13: 978-1492227755

ALSO BY SPIKE BLACK

Leave This Place
Avert Your Eyes
Ghost Ahead

For D.A.W.N.

DON'T
LOOK
INSIDE

HEED THE WARNING

CHAPTER 1

It was nothing, Lizzie convinced herself. *I'm not afraid.*

She snapped open her Zippo and held it up to her eyes, momentarily hypnotized by the allure of the dancing flame. But that familiar feeling of repulsion came over her and she closed the lighter. She settled back into the armchair and took a long drag on her marijuana cigarette.

Big, strange houses at night don't scare me.

She had long been of the opinion that smoking pot settled her nerves, calmed her down, made her invincible to fear. She studied the joint between her fingers.

Her hand was shaking.

It was a creak. Big deal. Old houses creak, you dumb bitch. Get over yourself.

Hell, she'd been in her newly-built apartment for ten months and already that place creaked like a hunched crone. But the fearful side of her brain, the larger, more dominant part, intervened.

Just a creak? Sure. Or a psychopath on the stairs.

Lizzie chuckled at her own stupidity. She puffed on her cigarette.

Her palms were moist with sweat.

This was insane. She'd been upstairs and there were no lurking psychopaths.

He's been waiting for you in the attic.

No, he hasn't.

He's at the bottom of the stairs now.

Fuck off.

Listen. You can hear him cackling in the hallway.

Don't. Please. She could feel a steady pulsing in her throat. *Just don't.*

It was nonsense. Of course it was. It was all in her head.

Forget about it. Chill your boots. Settle into your high.

She closed her eyes. Drew deeply. Took a moment.

Exhaled.

Goddammit.

Her eyes snapped open. She knew what she had to do.

She stepped into the hallway, recalling the words of her therapist, Fran: *Face your fears.*

It had been almost a year since the incident, and a change of county, a new town, a new life -

it had been good for her, had allowed her to move on, had almost, *almost* allowed her to forget. There were times when she had convinced herself that the events of that terrible night were erased from her memory. But, in truth, there were some things

(oh God, the window)

the very worst of things, that stayed with you.

Forever.

The hallway was lit only by the eerie glow of streetlights. The long branching shadows of windswept trees cavorted all around her.

Fear is only as deep as the mind will allow, Fran's silky tones informed her. She had been pretty, Fran, in a middle-aged, crow's feet and cardigans kind of way. And her dark-paneled office had smelled of leather and strawberries. Oh, how Lizzie longed to be back there.

She held out her dwindling cigarette like a pathetic spear - her only weapon. She jabbed at the air as she edged forward in the darkness. Surely not even psychopaths, she figured, enjoyed the sensation of burning eyeballs.

"Bring it on, asshole," she accidentally said out loud. She sounded tough, and she liked it. Nobody in their right mind, she was certain, would ever want to fuck with her.

But there was that voice again. *Psychopaths, on the whole, tend not to be right-minded individuals.*

It had a point.

There was another creaking noise, from

behind her this time. Her heart leapt.

She turned, slowly.

There, on the stairs.

Her blood ran cold. A figure in the dark.

She jumped, dropping her joint, and let slip a pathetic shriek.

A little girl, seven years old. Cute as anything.

Lizzie finally exhaled. "Christ, kid. You scared the crap out of me."

The little girl hugged her teddy bear tight to her chest. "That's a bad word."

"Yeah," Lizzie said. "I know a whole bunch of them. You wanna hear some more?"

***

Entering April's bedroom was like being assaulted by fairies. They were everywhere - on the wallpaper, on the lampshades, on a lantern by the bed - and Lizzie hated them, the winged pixie bitches.

She scanned the heaving bookshelf. "What does your mom normally read you?" She eyed the spines with contempt. Sparkly, shimmering books. Most of them, unsurprisingly, about fairies.

April sat in bed, propped up against a pile of pink pillows, waiting patiently. "My mommy doesn't read me stories. My daddy does."

"Duh." Kids were so dumb. "Your dad, whatever."

April explained that she had a whole bunch of

favorite books, and she liked to read them on rotation. Tonight was the turn of *The Wee Faerie Princess.*

Lizzie wasn't listening. Her attention was drawn to a leather-bound book. *Cat's Curiosity,* by Bertrand Powell. It was old, that was clear from the damage to the bottom of the spine, and the leather was a dull, pea-soup green, not screaming for attention like the other glitter-flecked atrocities.

Lizzie pulled the book from the shelf, the weight of it surprising her as she took it in both hands.

The cover itself had no title or author, merely an embossed illustration. At the center stood a little girl in a pinafore dress. Tree branches grew from her ears and flowed to the edges of the book, where they formed a frame for the cover, large apples hanging decoratively at the corners. The girl in the illustration did not appear to be disturbed by her leafy protuberances; on the contrary, she seemed delighted with them.

Lizzie looked closer. The girl's expression was partly obscured by scratches in the leather, but Lizzie could make out the narrowed eyes, the pinched nose, and the toothy, demonic grin.

The girl was staring directly at her.

Lizzie jolted, instinctively moving the book away. She thought of Fran.

Confront the things that scare you, each and every day, and soon you'll see that there's really nothing in this world to be frightened of at all.

"What about this?" Lizzie said, holding the book aloft for April to see.

The little girl craned her neck for a closer look. "What is it? I've never seen that before."

"Perfect." Lizzie carried the book over and sat on the end of the bed.

April pulled her covers up high. "It looks scary."

"You're too old to be afraid of stupid stories, aren't you?"

"I'm seven."

Lizzie secretly loved the idea of scaring this kid. She was too squeaky clean, with her fairies and pink pillows.

She opened the book to the first page. The paper was yellowing. It emitted a musty smell. She read aloud.

Cat was a curious little girl
With a pinafore dress and a cutesy curl.
She was ever so naughty for someone so young
And thought it funny to stick out her tongue.

"Stop that now," her mother said
"Or a bird will peck it out of your head."
Cat was curious; the thought made her giggle
So she stuck out her tongue and gave it a wiggle.

A blackbird watched from a nearby tree
Thinking her tongue was a worm for his tea.
Swooping, he pecked it off with his beak
And never again was Cat able to speak.

Lizzie curled her lip into a sneer. The creepy cover had promised so much more. "Totally lame."

April smiled. "I liked it."

"Yeah, you would."

April sulked. Lizzie didn't care. Even seven-year-olds should have standards. She glanced at the illustration on the facing page. A detailed drawing of a little girl in a pinafore dress, her tongue in the grip of an angry blackbird's beak. The girl looked eerily pleased at her predicament.

The picture made Lizzie's flesh crawl.

She closed the book. "Let's talk instead."

April brightened. She sat bolt upright. "Okay."

"What would you like to talk about?"

April thought for a moment. "What were you smoking downstairs? It didn't smell like my daddy's cigarettes."

Lizzie stared back at her, lost for words. She sighed. "We can always read a bit more, I suppose."

April cheered. Lizzie picked up the book.

Three words.

Scratched furiously into the leather of the cover.

DON'T
LOOK
INSIDE

Lizzie screamed. She jerked back.
What the hell?
The words were angry. A warning.

DON'T

Shrieking for her attention.

LOOK

She turned away.
"What is it?" April asked.
Lizzie cowered behind her hands. "Don't -"
She stopped herself.

She couldn't bring herself to say the words aloud. If she did, then that was an admission that they were real. But, of course, they were not real.

How could they be?

"I don't know," Lizzie cried. "I just don't know..."

Those three awful words had not been there when she had taken the book from the shelf. She was certain of that. But the way the letters had been scratched - with a sharp implement perhaps, or long fingernails, deep into the leather - it made no sense. How could the words have just appeared there? Her mind raced, grasping for a logical explanation.

It snagged one.

Rick the Dick.

That fucking prick.

Rick the Dick was Lizzie's name for her sister's boyfriend. He had also been her dealer before she skipped town.

That loser gave me some messed up shit.

It wouldn't be the first time. He gave her a pill in Ibiza; her fellow clubbers had become rubber-faced, wobbly-headed creatures, crowding around her, suffocating her, dancing like hungry demons in the eye-splitting strobe light.

She never called him Richard again after that experience.

Motherfucker. What had he done to her? Now she was seeing things. She wanted to slice off his balls.

She blinked hard. Rubbed her eyes. Picked up the book.

DON'T
LOOK
INSIDE

Still there. *Ah, fuck…*

Her heart hammered upward into her throat. Her legs jerked, pleading. *Let's get out of here.*

But her body stayed firm. *It's all in my mind. It's not real.*

April leaned in for a closer look. "Cool."

Lizzie gasped. "You can see that?"

"Of course."

An optical illusion, maybe. Or one of those trick covers where the writing reveals itself when tilted into the light. Lizzie ran her fingers over the letters. Carved deep into the leather.

This was no illusion.

DON'T
LOOK
INSIDE

She felt a desperate urge to look inside.

Her mind screamed one word.

No.

But her fingers compelled themselves on, grasping the edge of the cover.

Heed the warning.

Her hands were possessed. A mind of their own.

Stop. Please.

She absolutely did not want to look inside.

Or did she?

It begged the question - what actually was inside? Didn't she already know? Was there really anything more than just a crappy, rhyming children's book?

Besides, what was the worst that could happen? It was only a book, after all. It wasn't as if a lion or a ghost or a monster could leap out and devour her.

"Go on then," April said. "Open it."

That was all the encouragement Lizzie needed.

She flipped open the book.

CHAPTER 2

Words and pictures. That was all.

Lizzie's bottom lip jutted out, blowing cool air over the rough terrain of her cheeks. No bear trap had sprung from the book and chopped off her hands. Demons had not leapt from the pages and pulled her screaming into their fiery underworld.

"Read it," April insisted.

Words and pictures. They could do no harm.

Lizzie swallowed. Exhaled. Scanned the page.

Her relief turned to sudden horror.

Her breathing accelerated. Panic engulfed her mind like water filling a balloon. Her temples pulsed.

What have I done?

The first two words on the page.

Oh God, what have I done?

"What does it say?" April asked.

Lizzie was sure that it said a great deal. But

she was still fixated on those first two words. Two words that told her she was in a whole heap of trouble.

Her name.

DON'T LOOK INSIDE. It was a command, but also a come-on. Who could resist looking inside any book with those three words on the cover?

That was the point, though, Lizzie surmised.

It was a trap.

The book - or whatever supernatural entity had scratched those words into the leather - knew that nobody could resist a peek inside.

But this was personal. She had not anticipated that. The warning had been meant for her - specifically for her - all along. And that made the thought of reading on almost unbearably terrifying.

There's nothing to fear but fear itself.

The other voice in her head groaned in frustration. *Shut up, Fran.* Lizzie imagined strangling her with Fran's own string of pearls. Tightening the necklace around her scrawny throat. *Fear this, you bitch.*

April was losing patience. "What's going on? You're too old to be afraid of stupid stories, aren't you?"

The paralysis of terror subdued Lizzie's response. On any other evening her blood would have boiled at the cheek of the girl, but tonight she merely uttered a weak, "Nuh-uh."

She was currently distracted with other, more pressing concerns. She wondered if it was too late to go back. What were the rules of this sinister game? Once you looked inside, was it possible to *un*-look?

And yet still, her curiosity drove her on. Her name was written there. It was impossible to resist.

"What does it say?" April repeated, echoing Lizzie's own thoughts exactly.

She stared at those first two words.

Elizabeth Paul

That was her, all right. Nobody had called her by her full name for as long as she could remember. Except in the courtroom, of course. They had used it there. But it also happened to be quite a common name. So common, in fact, that at last count she had uncovered one-hundred and twenty-nine people called Elizabeth Paul on Facebook alone. It had made finding a unique username a real pain in the ass.

And it brought up a real interesting question. Could this whole thing just be one big coincidence? Maybe even a case of mistaken identity?

To hell with it. She read aloud.

Elizabeth Paul never bothered at school
Forever content to play the class fool.
She left with little education
And entered a world rife with temptation.

Lizzie's heart lurched. Her stomach twisted. This, she slowly realized as she read further, was not a case of mistaken identity.

Her prospects dim and her life on the skids
She thought, "Eureka! I'll work with young kids."
She faked the exams and hid her tattoos
Re-dyed her hair and bought sensible shoes.

Professional babysitting paid the bills
But it failed to offer the requisite thrills.
Soon an old habit reared its head
And in a puff of smoke, a girl was —

Lizzie choked on the last word.

She retched. Hot bile burned the back of her throat. She winced as she swallowed it back down again.

How was this possible?

The book...

It *knew.*

Her oldest, dearest, closest friends didn't know. Fran didn't know. Hell, even her parents didn't know *everything.* But somehow, this book...

"That story wasn't as good," April said. "Maybe the next one will be better."

But Lizzie refused to read aloud any longer. Story time was over. She stared intently at the words, wanting to read on, but so very afraid. What else did the book know?

And in a puff of smoke, a girl was dead.

Panic roared in her mind.

The truth.

She had lied so much about what had happened that night that she had started to believe the lies herself. The truth was a brutal shock even to her.

(oh God, the window)

She couldn't face the truth. Not now, not ever.

She threw the book down and scampered to the other side of the room.

"What are you doing?" April shouted.

Lizzie buried her hands in her hair. She paced, her skin crawling, her legs itching.

How? How could it know?

An overwhelming feeling of despair came over her. She whimpered.

April looked down at the book on the floor. She was curious. She picked it up.

Lizzie looked back just as the book fell open to a random page.

"No!"

She dived across the room, but it was too late. April pulled the book away from her grasping hands.

"Stop!" Lizzie commanded. "You mustn't!"

April didn't take orders from babysitters. Especially crazy ones. And besides, didn't this silly woman know anything? In *The Big Book of Babysitting,* rule number one stated: *Never say the word* mustn't *to a seven-year-old. It will only encourage them.*

April rolled away from Lizzie and read aloud.

Cat was a curious little girl
With a pinafore dress and a cutesy curl.
She was pretty and sweet when she wanted to be
But she'd rather pull faces and look ugly.

Lizzie was intrigued. "Let me see that." She reached for the book, but April rolled away again.

"Ooh, this book is *so* scary," April said.

"You brat! Give me that, now!"

April ignored her and continued reading.

Her mother said "Cat, stop being a twit
Or the wind will change and you'll stay like it."
Cat was curious; could it be true?
So she pulled a face that belonged in the zoo.

She climbed a hilltop and waited forever
For even the slightest change in the weather.
Then the wind did change, and Cat did gurn
Now wherever she goes she makes stomachs turn.

April laughed.

Lizzie ran around to the other side of the bed. "This is not a game, kid. This is serious." She snatched the book away. Checked the cover.

Nothing but the embossed illustration.

She flipped it over. Turned it back again. This made no sense.

The warning had vanished, just as suddenly

as it had appeared. She placed her hand over the leather where the deeply carved letters had been only minutes earlier.

Was it possible? Could it have all been in her mind?

Was that why the book knew things? Because it had been her imagination all along? But what about April? She claimed she had seen the warning. Had she lied?

Or maybe Rick the Dick's pot was so potent, it messed with your head through second hand smoke alone...

Lizzie checked the verses in the book. They were exactly as April had read aloud. She glanced over at the illustration on the facing page.

The little girl in the pinafore dress stared back at her, her fingers stretching her mouth hideously wide, her facial features mangled. The look in her eyes was one of maniacal delight.

Lizzie shivered. She slammed the book shut. Dust particles danced in the air.

The cover began to move before her eyes.

The material ripped. A puncture hole appeared.

"No, no..."

The hole widened as an invisible hand carved deep into the leather.

D - O

She dropped down onto the bed. She watched, mesmerized, as more letters appeared.

DON'T

Then beneath that, scratched quickly:

LOOK

April screamed.

Lizzie hadn't even noticed the girl watching over her shoulder. "You can see that?"

"Yes, yes." April's voice trembled. "I can see that."

Well, you succeeded, the voice in Lizzie's head piped up. *You finally scared the girl good, just like you wanted.*

I - N - S -

Lizzie didn't wait for it to finish.

"Fuck *this!*" she screamed. "Bring it on! I am *not* afraid!"

April was stunned. "Language!"

Lizzie pulled open the book.

April hid behind her hands. She couldn't resist a peek between her fingers.

New words now. A new illustration.

April leaned in closer, pressing against Lizzie's back. "That looks like my room."

Lizzie studied the picture. Sure enough, there was a drawing of the fairy lantern on the nightstand. And the full-length mirror by the closet. And the window out to the balcony. In the foreground two figures sat on the bed, engrossed in a book. A woman and a young girl. The girl was peering over the woman's shoulder.

It's as if, Lizzie thought with encroaching dread, *somebody has drawn a sketch of this exact moment.*

She read aloud the first verse.

"Read me a story," April said
In her fairy pajamas on her fairy bed.
But Lizzie hated the books on the shelves
About princesses and pixie elves.

"That's like us," April said.

Lizzie shivered. Goosebumps rippled down her flesh. "Yes. Yes, that's very much like us."

She found a dark and creepy story
Just suitably scary - nothing gory.
But soon she wished she'd picked another
When words carved deep into the cover.

All the muscles in Lizzie's body tightened at once. "I can't do this."

"This is awesome," April said.

Despite her fear, Lizzie was already reading ahead. "Wait - listen to this."

'Don't Look Inside' the message warned
Lizzie worried; April yawned.
What was inside? It made you wonder
Now right on cue: a crash of thunder.

April gasped. Lizzie turned to her. They locked eyes in the heavy silence.

April's mouth dropped open. Lizzie winced and gritted her teeth.

They waited.

An explosion of thunder boomed from the heavens.

They jumped and screamed in unison. Lizzie clamped her hands to her mouth. Her eyes welled with tears.

April jumped up and down on the bed. "What else does it say? What else does it say?"

Lizzie laughed just as a tear trickled down her cheek. She couldn't help herself. She understood the young girl's excitement. She, too, couldn't wait to keep reading, despite feeling more terrified than she had been in her entire life.

April giggled. They looked at one another, and smiled. Lizzie felt seven-years-old again. She wondered if it were beyond the realms of possibility that they could ever be friends.

April looked down at the book. Her expression changed instantly.

Lizzie saw the fear mounting on April's face. She felt sick. *Oh, no. What now?*

April pointed to the illustration with a

hesitant finger. "Who…is that?"

Those three words turned Lizzie's heart to ice. She really, *really* didn't want to look. But her neck turned anyway, and her eyes glanced down at the book, and she saw.

There was somebody else in the drawing. Lizzie hadn't noticed before. She looked closer.

A dark figure at the window.

The silhouette of a woman with long hair.

Lizzie gasped. She looked up from the book. Out of the rain-spattered window. She could see only darkness. She looked harder.

A sudden spark of blue-white lightning revealed a figure, standing there. Outside the window. A face pressed up to the glass. A twisted, angry face. A woman with long hair.

Staring in at them.

She was there only for the duration of the lightning flash. Then she was gone again. Sucked back into the blackness of the night.

April screamed before Lizzie had a chance to react. "Somebody's out there!"

A bolt of cold fear shot through Lizzie's body. *No shit.*

She couldn't stand it any longer. She sprung to her feet, clutching the book. She marched across the room, headed straight for the window. "Don't worry babe, nothing's there," she said, her voice breaking. "Nothing. Nothing at all."

She focused on the swirling pattern of the curtains as she reached out and yanked them shut. She could not allow herself to think about what was outside, in the darkness, on the other side of the thin pane of glass.

There is nothing to fear but fear itself.

Yeah, Lizzie thought. *Thanks, Fran. If it's not too much trouble, I'd like a refund please.*

What the *hell* was that thing out there? Her arms prickled. She could feel its presence.

She spoke slowly. "April - do me a favor, okay? Whatever you do, don't move from the bed."

April shot beneath the covers and bunched them up under her chin. She began to cry.

Lizzie tried to concentrate amidst the fog of fears clogging her mind. What next? She looked down at the book in her hand. *Of course.* The book would tell her. Just maybe, if she did the opposite of what the book had in store for them, she could get through this nightmare.

She turned the page.

The illustration was a simple, black square of nothing.

What could *that* mean?

There was a buzz of electricity as the lights flickered, and suddenly Lizzie knew.

Oh, no.

The book slipped from her hand, crashing to the floor. The lights extinguished with a pop. The room was plunged into darkness. The house fell silent.

April cried louder.

Lizzie froze. Her heart slammed in her ears. The squeal of the wind outside the window had intensified.

She felt horribly exposed in the dark, as if she was being watched by something with perfect night vision. She clambered through the black, her arms outstretched, her feet shuffling. The floorboards creaked with every step forward. Her fingers found the wall, then the hinges of the door. She groped around for the light switch.

That thing. That woman. She was probably here, pressed up against the wall. Lizzie felt sure that she was going to touch her as she fumbled around in the dark. Any moment now, in her haste to find the switch, she was going to grab onto a bony arm. She knew exactly what it would feel like: cold and slimy like a freshly-caught fish, and rippling with tight veins.

She shuddered. *Stop it.*

And then it happened. The woman seized her hand. The merciless grip crushed Lizzie's bones, the sharp talons of its nails digging deep into the tender meat of her palms —

Pack it in. Seriously. Her imagination was astonishingly vivid in the dark. For a moment it really had felt like something had reached out and grabbed her wrist.

Lizzie found the switch. She flicked it.

Nothing.

"It's okay, babe. Just a power cut." *Wow.* She couldn't believe how cool and calm she sounded. *And the Oscar goes to...*

Rain battered at the window. Or was it the woman's fingers tapping on the glass? Lizzie's entire body stiffened, the tension in her bones causing a dull ache that rose from her ankles and dissipated somewhere around her lower back. She felt around in her pocket and pulled out the Zippo lighter. She flicked it open.

The flame illuminated a wedge of the room a few feet ahead. She turned slowly in a circle, checking all around her.

The woman stood in the corner, her eyes glinting in the dark.

No. It was a shade on a tall lamp stand. Lizzie's heart restarted. She breathed again.

April poked her head out from beneath the covers, tears streaming down her face.

"It's okay," Lizzie said, approaching the nightstand. "Everything will be okay." She was aware that she was comforting herself as much as the little girl. She opened the small hinged door on the fairy lantern. With a trembling hand she lit the wick of the candle inside. The fairies on the lantern cover appeared to dance in the light of the flickering flame.

She picked up the book, its pages still splayed open. Her fingertips ran along the indentations made by the scratches of the words in the cover. *Like caressing the hand of a demon,* she thought, and shuddered. She turned the page and tried to read by the lantern light. She couldn't make out the words. She snapped open her lighter. Its eerie flame illuminated the pages perfectly.

Her eyes darted to the illustration. A picture-perfect large family house. A row of tall sunflowers peering over the top of a picket fence.

The house was on fire. Enormous, bright orange flames billowed from the windows. To Lizzie's tired eyes they seemed as real as the flame she held in her hand. They appeared, almost, to flicker...

Something else drew her attention. On the upper level of the house, through the blaze, Lizzie could just about make out —

(oh God, the window)

Lizzie's stomach rolled. Her body heaved. She clamped a hand to her mouth. A muffled howl escaped through her fingers.

No. Please no...

CHAPTER 3

Lizzie was baked.

Her skin sizzled in the midday sun. The dance music pumping through her earbuds whisked her mind back to the intense partying of the night before.

The heat was almost unbearable by the poolside, far hotter even than it had been on the dance floor. She knew it got like this in the Mediterranean around early afternoon, but still - this was something else.

She needed a break. Then again, it had to be lunch soon anyway. She could smell the patio barbecue.

The air was thin. The music in her ears was getting annoyingly repetitive.

Beep. Beep. Beep. Beep.

The same ear-bursting squeal, over and over. And that smell - she must have been downwind of the barbecue, because the smoke was getting up her nose.

God, the heat. She couldn't stand it.

She gasped for air, but there was none. She coughed. Her skin fried. The noise in her ears grew louder.

Beep. Beep. Beep. Beep.

She had to move.

Get out of the sun.

She was choking. She couldn't breathe. Like, for real. She seriously could not breathe —

Her eyes snapped open.

She was not at the villa in Ibiza.

A swirling pattern of gray smoke shifted across a plastered ceiling. Her head throbbed.

Where the hell am I?

She tried to swallow, but her throat was raw.

Beep. Beep. Beep. Beep.

That noise again. *Make it stop -*

A fire alarm.

She sat bolt upright. Through the haze she could make out a living room. This wasn't her apartment. The arm of the couch melted beneath her hand.

She stumbled to her feet, coughing. Pulled her shirt up, clamping it around her mouth and nose to create a makeshift air filter.

Beneath the piercing scream of the alarm there was another constant sound. Crackling.

A photo in a large gold frame hung on the wall. A family portrait. She didn't recognize anyone in the picture. Maybe the little girl, but…no.

The glass popped and splintered in the frame.

She jumped. Turned, looking for a way out.

Light escaped from the edges of a door. She moved cautiously toward it. The soles of her sneakers stuck to the carpet and tore away with each step.

As she neared the door, flames appeared through the smoke, lapping at the walls in bright sheets, blistering the art deco crescents of the wallpaper.

She grabbed the door handle. The metal was hot.

White hot. It seared into her palm.

She ripped her hand away, yelping like a wounded mutt, her skin remaining behind. Coating the handle like a film of dried glue.

She levered the door open with a sneaker and pushed through into the hallway.

BEEP. BEEP. BEEP. BEEP.

Streetlights. Through the mottled glass of the front door.

She headed in that direction, coughing uncontrollably. The unforgiving shriek of the alarm pierced her skull.

A rolling blanket of fire ascended the stairs to her left.

A light fixture dropped and smashed.

Sparks swirled in the air around her. She patted at her hair, convinced it was alight.

The house groaned as its timbers contracted.

She couldn't breathe. She collapsed to her knees.

BEEP. BEEP. BEEP. BEEP.

Wait.

Another noise.

Hammering.

Yes. Hammering at the front door. She looked up, her eyes stinging and streaming as she struggled to see through the gloom.

The glass in the door pane shattered. An arm reached in and flipped the lock.

Blackness.

Weightlessness.

She was being lifted under her arms. Over the threshold. The toes of her sneakers brushed the welcome mat.

Outside now.

The fresh air hit her lungs. Nothing ever tasted so good.

She was out.

Saved.

A miracle.

Her feet landed on concrete. She tried walking, but her legs were jelly.

She felt bad for her poor rescuer, having to support most of her weight as she hobbled down the garden path. *Thank you,* she tried to say, in a hoarse whine that was not her voice. *Thank you, thank you!*

People.

Lots of them.

Most of the neighborhood.

Standing around, watching.

Wait a minute…

She recognized this street. She knew this place. She was here regularly.

A female onlooker screamed. Pointed back at the house. "Oh God, the window…"

The woman's face was a mask of pure horror.

Lizzie turned back, craning her neck, looking up, following the direction of the woman's outstretched arm.

A second floor window. Too bright for Lizzie to see clearly. Shouting from onlookers.

A tiny, blackened hand punctured the glare of the flames and flattened against the window pane with a thud.

In a dizzying wave of realization, Lizzie remembered exactly where she was.

Someone in that family portrait had looked familiar.

The little girl.

Daisy Reynolds.

Her Tuesday job.

Somewhere in the back of her mind, Lizzie registered the faint wail of approaching sirens.

They were too late.

She fell to the ground, screaming, hiding her face so that she wouldn't have to watch as little Daisy Reynolds burned.

CHAPTER 4

Lizzie stared at the illustration for so long that when she screwed her eyes shut the image had seared itself onto the backs of her eyelids.

A little girl. Helpless. Her arms aloft, her tiny body consumed by flames.

Lizzie reopened her eyes, her heart filled with dread. She fought the automatic compulsion to read the words on the page, but something inside drove her attention there anyway.

She escaped her room, but died on the stairs
Now that crispy girl is the stuff of nightmares.
And all because, in your spaced-out haze
You dropped your spliff and caused a blaze.

Your secret was safe; no proof came to light
But you knew the truth in the dead of night.
The judge bought your lies; no charges were filed
No blame brought to bear for the death of a child.

And so you skipped town, to start life afresh
But still you smelled her burning flesh.
Quit running Elizabeth, for now it's time
You'll pay for your despicable crime.

Lizzie felt a strange calmness wash over her as she read the words.

Quit running, Elizabeth

She was glad.

All the joy of living had drained from her soul since that awful night. She had been unable to work, or socialize, or take a holiday, or relax into a hobby, or concentrate on basic everyday tasks. Not once since had she enjoyed an ice cream in the park, or lost herself in the plot of a good book, or felt any degree of love for another human being. Most days were spent on the couch in her apartment, watching daytime TV and smoking pot with the curtains closed.

Her favorite time of day was the first few seconds after waking. Before it all came flooding back.

She took the page between her fingers and prepared to turn it.

She crossed herself. Whispered a prayer. Pulled a crucifix from her shirt and kissed it.

I'm ready. Do what you will.

She flipped the page.

Despite the guilt, you haven't learned
Nothing's changed since Daisy burned.
So pack up all hope and quit your prayers
For tonight another girl dies on the stairs.

Her eyes widened. For a moment she was frozen in shock.

"No, no, NO!" she cried. "You can't do this!"

April uncurled herself from the sheets. "Can't do what?"

"It's against the rules," Lizzie exclaimed to the ceiling, her arms outstretched. "Leave her alone!"

April swung her legs over the edge of the bed. "Lizzie, you're scaring me."

"Stay in bed. Please, honey. Don't move. For God's sake, don't move."

Her eyes darted frantically over the lines of the verse again.

For tonight another girl dies on the stairs.

She studied the words, trying to allow them past the wall of fear that had erected in her mind.

Girl.

Stairs.

Fire.

She gasped, looking over at the naked flame in her hand.

She watched in horror as the lighter slipped from her grasp.

It seemed to fall in slow motion. Onto the bed.

The lid closed with a snap, extinguishing the flame. Lizzie batted frantically at the bedsheets anyway.

She picked up the lighter by her fingertips and hurled it across the room. It smacked hard against the radiator, making a horrible clanging noise that echoed around the room.

April dived under the duvet.

Lizzie covered her ears.

What else? She whipped left, then right.

The lantern.

Must blow out the candle.

She opened the little door. Hesitated.

She needed its illumination to read the book.

Get it away from her.

She closed the door and picked up the lantern by its handle.

Stepped precariously over to the pink fairy rug in the center of the room. Threw down the book. Kneeled on the rug and held the lantern over the words.

Her heart hammered in her chest.

She turned the page.

Why bother trying? You can't change fate
For that it's much too fucking late.
You were warned - Don't Look Inside
Now there's nowhere left to hide.

Lizzie fixated on the words. A whimper escaped her lips.

She knew she would have to check out the illustration on the facing page, but she was paralyzed with fear.

She read the verse through again. Took a deep breath.

She glanced at the picture.

She saw a representation of herself, kneeling on the rug, holding the lantern over the book.

And in the full-length mirror by the closet was the reflection of a sinister figure.

Lizzie's stomach rolled. She looked up.

She was there, reflected in the mirror.

The woman.

She appeared to be looking at herself, but only her reflection could be seen.

She was much easier on the eye than Lizzie had expected. Long red hair. Pretty.

Her eyes flicked across, locking on Lizzie.

Her head followed, turning sharply.

Her face changed.

It distorted into a rotting scowl so violent and terrible that as Lizzie gazed upon it she knew, with unwavering certainty, that her life was about to end.

She shrieked and dropped the lantern.

The tea light inside rolled around on its edge. The little door flapped open.

Lizzie dropped to her knees. She reached for the lantern, but it was too late. She could only watch as the candle toppled out, its flame hitting the rug.

NO!

She batted at the burning fabric, pummeling a cute fairy's blackened face until the flame extinguished.

Charred embers frolicked in the air.

It was over. Lizzie exhaled.

Her sleeves ignited.

She screamed, waving her arms hopelessly as the flames spread. She toppled toward the bed.

April screamed and backed away.

Must protect the girl.

Lizzie turned and ran for the door.

April peered out from beneath her covers just as Lizzie bolted from the room, leaving a wisp of smoke in her wake.

The girl wrapped the bedsheets around her head. She hugged her teddy bear tight to her chest. The world was muffled now. So muffled, in fact, that she barely heard Lizzie's agonized screams, or the series of terrible thudding noises that immediately followed.

CHAPTER 5

Sergeant Della Kirby slammed the door of her patrol car and dashed for the house, sheltering her face from the driving rain. She ran up the steps and nodded to the officer standing guard at the entrance. *Kevin*, she thought. It was something like that.

Kevin - *Kelvin?* - opened the door for her. She stepped inside.

The smell assaulted her immediately, bringing with it a rush of images. She pushed them away. *Not now.*

They were persistent, as only the most terrible memories were. Still frames, soundtracked by shrill screams. She shook her head violently, an attempt to rid her mind of their vile allure. Afterimages remained, encouraged by that lingering and unmistakable odor, but they hung around only until Della saw the body on the stairs.

A fresh new horror.

A bitter taste in the mouth.

"Della," the man kneeling over the body said. "We really must stop meeting like this."

"I know. Tell me about it."

Della liked Harlan, the coroner's deputy. He had an easy way about him. He was one of the few friends she had made since arriving in England. Chalkstone was a quiet town, and the people seemed friendly enough, but they kept to themselves. Della wondered if the day would ever come when she'd stop feeling like an outsider.

"Almost holiday time, isn't it?" Harlan said. "Or should I say, 'vacation'."

"Just the night shift to go. I fly out tomorrow lunchtime."

"Lucky you. I'm so envious. I've always wanted to see the East Coast."

Della and her sister had been planning this road trip forever. She remembered drawing up an itinerary when she was a cadet in Boston, and the only thing that had changed almost two decades later was the timeframe. They had hoped to do it all in six weeks, but she'd had to keep delaying until she'd saved up enough vacation time.

Now, though, Thanksgiving was little more than a month away, and neither of them wanted to be on the road that weekend. Which meant it was going to have to be a whistle-stop tour. But wasn't that the point of these trips? Besides, she was mostly looking forward to going back home. Spending some quality time with Donna. They hadn't seen each other since she'd transferred overseas, and they had a lot of catching up to do.

Della fished a pair of disposable gloves from her pocket. "So, what have we got?"

"Her name's Elizabeth Paul. Twenty-three. Possible head injuries, but no obvious fractures. Superficial burns to the hands."

The girl's head hung upside down from the bottom stair. Della twisted to get a good look at her. The pull of gravity made it look like Elizabeth's hair was standing on end.

As if she had seen a ghost.

Elizabeth had weathered skin. A stud in her nose. Frown lines creased her brow. For a girl so young, the years had not been kind. Tough life, Della surmised, and most likely not in this respectable neighborhood.

"Au pair?"

"Babysitter. Parents aren't home yet. Girl's upstairs with an officer."

Della sighed. She glanced up the staircase that trailed off into a blanket of darkness. Poor kid. The trauma she must have been through. Her stomach twisted. She couldn't stand to see children that way.

Della stepped away from the body, surveying the scene. She saw something on the floor in the hallway. She picked it up. The cause of that familiar smell - a joint.

"Not now," Harlan said. "I'm working."

A picture of the night's events began to form in Della's mind. Elizabeth Paul, it did not take the world's greatest detective to figure out, was an irresponsible babysitter. She had spent the evening getting high. Her young charge had been unable to sleep, had called for her; Elizabeth had stumbled up the flight of stairs, but by this time was barely lucid. On her way back down, the polished bannister would have looked inviting. Maybe she had tried to slide down it.

"Was it the fall that killed her?"

"I'll be able to tell you more at autopsy," Harlan said. "Her neck's not broken, but with a tumble like this you'd be looking at internal injuries. Probable head trauma."

Della stared into the frozen pools of Lizzie's eyes. She felt a flash of icy terror.

The faces of the dead had followed her across the Atlantic.

"There's something else you need to take a look at," Harlan said.

"Oh?"

Harlan pulled aside the collar of Lizzie's shirt. Lifted her necklace.

Della leaned in. Terrible burn marks circled Lizzie's neck. A deep furrow indented the skin through the center of the burns.

Della winced. "Rope marks?"

"They're recent, but they're not the cause of death. I'd guess maybe twenty-four hours."

"She did it herself?"

Harlan nodded. "Her injuries are consistent with suicidal hanging."

Della was overcome with a feeling of pity for the girl. *Your life was tougher than we'll ever know.*

She felt that cold terror again, and this time it didn't go away quite so quickly.

CHAPTER 6

Della found the kid in her bedroom. A female officer was comforting her.

"April?"

The girl looked up. The red rings around her eyes contrasted greatly against the deathly pallor of her skin.

"I'm Della."

The girl's voice trembled. "Lizzie said whatever I do, I mustn't move from the bed."

Della's heart ached for her. "It's okay, sweetie. You're safe. You can move now."

April stayed stiff as a board.

Della knelt down beside her. The girl flinched. "It's okay," Della repeated. She took the girl's hand in her own. It was cold as ice. "You think you can tell me about Lizzie's accident?"

Incredulity flickered across April's face. "It wasn't an accident."

Della raised her eyebrows. "What do you mean?"

April hesitated. She pointed to the floor.

Della looked around. "The book?"

She nodded.

Della reached for it, noting the rug with a burned hole through it where a fairy's head had been.

"No!" April yelled as Della's hand touched the cover. The girl began to cry.

"Ssh, ssh. It's okay. What did you want to tell me about the book?"

April grabbed Della's wrists and squeezed tight. She stared deep into her eyes. "Please. Don't. Don't look inside." Tears tumbled down her cheeks.

Della smiled reassuringly. She wriggled free from her grasp and grabbed the book. "But it's already open. See?"

The girl recoiled with a gasp. "No! Keep it away!"

Della studied the illustration on the page. A grubby-faced little girl in a pinafore dress stared back, her fingers pulling her mouth wide, her tongue lolling out. Her eyes were wild and dangerous.

Della turned the page.

"No!" the girl cried.

"It's fine, April. I'm just checking it out, okay?"

She stroked the girl's hair, calming her. She flicked through the book. It was old and impressively bound, but in a sorry state. Pages were torn and stained. Clearly, this book had been popular with generations of children. She skimmed through the verses of one of the stories. In it, the girl's mother warned her not to poke her belly button or her bottom would fall off. The girl defied her mother and did it anyway. The consequences were predictable.

Della closed the book. The cover was decorated with an illustration in the scratched leather. An apple tree grew from the little girl's ears.

She checked the spine. *Cat's Curiosity*, by Bertrand Powell.

April studied her with wide eyes, awaiting the verdict.

"Shall I let you into a little secret?" Della said. "This book totally freaks me out."

April's mouth dropped open.

"And that's because I have a big imagination. It's a creepy little book, for sure. But you and me - we're the same. What's there on the page really isn't all that frightening, but we make it scarier in our heads."

She offered the book to April. The girl took it. She flicked through the pages.

"See?" She dried the girl's cheek. "It's just a book."

April closed the book and checked the cover. Ran her hand over the leather.

She reopened it. Showed Della the drawing of the little girl sticking her tongue out. Della copied the picture and stuck her tongue out, too. April giggled.

"Now," Della said. "Why don't we start from the beginning? Tell me exactly what happened."

CHAPTER 7

Chalkstone Police Station was a handsome Victorian building perched at the top of a hill on the north end of the High Street. Unlike many structures of its age it had retained the purpose for which it had originally been built. Della found this to be a mixed blessing, for the station was both perfectly preserved and hideously outdated. She loved that she got to work inside such an old building - it felt very English, very proper, and it matched many of the preconceived ideas she'd had about working as a police officer in the British Isles. But it was also rather frustrating.

Something as simple as making an arrest in the town had become a trial, given that there was no longer a functioning custody department at the station. The cell block had been decommissioned in the early nineties, having failed to meet safety regulations. Too many young offenders had hanged themselves from the water pipes that snaked the ceilings of the cells, or had been found dangling from the light fittings, or had seen fit to end it all with a leap from the spiked railings that made up the roof of the exercise yard.

This had resulted in the current and, Della felt, faintly ridiculous situation whereby if she arrested someone in Chalkstone, she would have to take them to the neighboring Eldham station to be processed. A time-consuming procedure that had irked many of her fellow officers. She had not failed to notice a sharp decline in arrests and a vast increase in street warnings in her short time here.

Della busied herself in her office on the upper floor, filling in forms and faxing them to the coroner. It was all she could do not to think about the fact that she was the only officer in the station. It was three in the morning, it was colder inside than out, and the world on the other side of the window pane was, from her vantage point, nothing but a silent and devastating blackness, the night sky devoid of stars.

Back in the days when she'd patrolled the Fenwick Park area of Boston, Della had lived in a tiny room downtown that her landlord once generously described as a studio apartment. The view from her only window consisted of red brick and the last two letters of a neon HOTEL sign on the neighboring building. Even with the blinds closed, the flaming orange EL of the sign would continue to taunt her, winking on and off endlessly, all night, every night.

How very apt, she would think, as she lay there listening to the constant hum of the city, accompanied by its orchestra of screams, shouts and sirens on the streets below. *My own waking EL.*

The view from her office window in Chalkstone made Della nostalgic for those days.

Her office backed onto flat, featureless Suffolk countryside, meaning that even in daylight hours there was very little worth seeing. But on moonless nights such as this she often found herself staring out into an empty black void, a view that almost always inspired dark, existential thoughts - matters she generally avoided thinking about, like the fragile nature of life and the cold inevitability of death. The stuff that used to send a chill through her heart as a teenager, when she awoke sometimes in the middle of the night.

Around this time of night, in fact.

Della shivered.

She filed away the forms, wondering what she could do next to occupy her mind. Her colleagues always managed to avoid being left alone in the station on the graveyard shift, preferring to be stuck in custody at Eldham station, or to be scouring the streets aimlessly. And ordinarily, Della was fine with that.

The random creaks and moans of the building did not make her think of haunted houses, despite the regular protestations of Trish on the front desk. She had never been spooked by the countless tales, told by immature male officers, of the ghosts that supposedly roamed the corridors. Sure, the building was old and creepy, and the way the heavy door outside her office randomly opened and closed sometimes was kind of strange, but this place, on the whole, had never frightened her.

Until tonight.

That stupid book had gotten to her.

No. Not the book.

There *had* been something supremely wrong about the expression on the face of the girl in the illustrations, but no, it wasn't the book. She could cope with the book.

It was April's reaction to it. She had been so… *convinced.*

A prickle of fear needled the back of her neck.

Anyway…

Keep busy, Della told herself.

She called the control room and asked them to contact the neighboring force. Elizabeth's parents would receive an agony message from two of Cambridgeshire's finest within the hour, and it made Della's stomach roll just thinking about it. For only the second time in her adult life she was relieved that she did not yet have children.

She updated the job on the system. Before long, she found her mind wandering to thoughts of home. She liked this job; even loved it on occasion - the thrill of working in another country, the more relaxed pace, the joy of not having to carry a weapon and worry that at any time she might have to use it - but she missed home, she missed her family, and boy, did she need a break. She had always been the type of person to throw herself into her work, to obsess over it at the expense of all other aspects of her life, and even she recognized when it was time for a vacation.

Screeee—screeee—screeee—screeee—

Della jumped.

She recognized that shrill squeal instantly, and her whole body tightened. *No. Not tonight, please…*

Screeee—screeee—screeee—screeee—

The cell alarm.

Despite being condemned twenty years earlier, the custody block still had an active cell alarm. It consisted of a rubber strip set into a metal casing that ran around the walls of the cells and the custody desk, just above eye level. It had made it easier for officers to reach up and call for assistance in cases of emergency.

Back then, the alarm had been connected to the control room, but not anymore. There was no call for an alarm on the cell block nowadays, and yet here it was, that piercing screech, invading her brain and swelling the reach of her already persistent headache.

There was, of course, no reason for the alarm to activate at all, given that there was nobody down there. The place was empty.

Or at least, it was *supposed* to be.

Screeee—screeee—screeee—screeee—

Della's skin prickled again.

Okay. Whatever.

She headed out of the office and down the dark corridor. She saw the reset key in her mind; it was on a control panel behind the custody desk. If she wanted that infernal noise to stop, and given the pulsing throb in her temples she very much did, then she had no option.

She would have to go down there.

The alarm had activated once before that she remembered, but she had not been alone in the station on that occasion, and it had not been the middle of the night. She later discovered that it had been Kelvin - or was it Kevin? - Hayes, the devilish little prankster, trying his best to spook everyone at the station, and succeeding for the most part.

But Kelvin's shift had finished at two, and Della thought it unlikely that any of her fellow officers on shift with her tonight would have the balls to sneak down to the cell block for what was - *sorry, Kelvin* - a pretty weak practical joke. Wendy? No way. And certainly not Silas. Despite being an enormous guy - over six feet tall and half as wide - he was terrified of the place. He refused point blank to ever go down there.

Della passed through the heavy door that led into the staircase and heard it *kaa-frumph* behind her. It was an unmistakable and very familiar sound, one that she had heard on multiple occasions while sitting at her desk. Every time she had lifted her head expecting someone to pass by in the corridor, and when nobody appeared she always felt a chill run through her.

That door liked to *kaa-frumph* on its own sometimes, it seemed.

She had attributed it to an updraft from the staircase. As she descended the stairs, feeling no draft whatsoever, she began to wonder if all this time there had been another, more supernatural explanation...

Stupid woman.

She had never been one to be suckered in by talk of the paranormal. She had witnessed too many real world horrors to let that be an issue. It had just been a long night, that was all. As she stepped off the staircase and approached the door to the cell block she concluded that April had most likely invented the whole 'haunted book' thing as a way to try and justify what had happened to Elizabeth. Kids' minds worked like that.

She pulled open the door and headed inside.

SCREEEE—SCREEEE—SCREEEE—SCREEE—

So loud now.

She flipped the light switch and waited, staring into the void of darkness.

The lights flickered on and then off again, illuminating the cell block for the briefest moment.

The door clicked shut, locking behind her.

She felt a hot flush of panic.

Checked the bunch of keys on her waistband.

Yes, she still had the plastic keycard that would allow her exit. She really should have checked that first; she did not want to be locked in here all night.

The lights flickered once more and stayed on this time, bathing the cell block in a sickly yellow glow. Combined with her relentless headache, it made her feel decidedly queasy. And that goddamned alarm…

She put out a hand to steady herself. Shattered plaster broke from the wall and crumbled beneath her palm.

The custody desk was ahead of her. The cell corridor was hidden from view on the right. She marched over to the desk. Peered behind it. Turned and headed down the corridor.

There was a broken light at the far end; the final cells were hard to make out. She passed the juvenile cell and peered in through its large viewing window. The cell was occupied, but only by the rows of file boxes stored there.

There were nine remaining cells, four on each side of the narrow aisle and one on its own at the far end. She approached the hatch built into the door of the first cell. She hesitated for a brief moment, then grabbed hold of the lip at the bottom of the flap.

Red letters were stamped into the metal: *KEEP THIS HATCH CLOSED*. She pulled it open anyway.

An empty cell, consisting of a basic bunk and a small window that projected a grid pattern of light onto one of the bare stone walls. She leaned in for a closer look.

Had she been the scream queen protagonist of a horror film, then at precisely this moment a crazed lunatic would have sprung from beneath the rectangle of her limited view and given her the fright of her life.

But nothing of the sort happened. Because this was reality.

More than that, it was Chalkstone. A dozy little town so ingrained in the banal it was almost stifling. Perhaps that was why the night's events had had such an effect on her: she simply wasn't conditioned to expect such *drama*.

She checked the rest of the cells quickly, passing the overpainted doors, sliding open the hatches, peering in. A quick glance was enough. A broken printer and an old computer monitor in one cell. A bank of filing cabinets in another.

Only one cell left now, emerging from the cloak of darkness.

Solitary.

It was maybe five feet apart from the other cells but it seemed to take many more steps for Della to reach it, somehow. As if it was stretching farther back the closer she got.

Her pace slowed as she approached the hatch. There was a sudden and inexplicable chill in the air. The smell of damp was stronger now.

No. Not damp.

Something more pungent. Something… wrong.

The smell of rotting flesh, maybe.

She put her fingers to the cold metal lip of the hatch.

KEEP THIS HATCH CLOSED.

She could almost feel April's icy little hands clutching at her wrists. Trembling. Squeezing. Her watery eyes pleading.

Please. Don't.

Don't look inside.

Fear twisted like a writhing snake in her belly.

SCREEEE—SCREEEE—SCREEEE—SCREEEE—

She froze.

Why do this to herself? There was clearly nothing down here. Nobody was hiding in the cells. The alarm was busted, and had been for some time.

She dropped her hand away from the hatch. Turned and headed back the way she had come, toward the custody desk.

She heard footsteps behind her.

Or at least, she *thought* she heard footsteps behind her. But that would be ridiculous. She snapped her head around and checked. Just in case.

Nothing. It must have been the echo of her own boots on the linoleum.

For a nanosecond she was afraid to turn back and face the way she was headed because *that* was when horror movies made the audience shriek by having the heroine slam into something unexpected. But she turned her head anyway, and once again there was nothing.

What the hell is wrong with me?

She snuck behind the custody desk and scanned the control panel. A swell of panic *(there* is *no key!)* subsided as she found what she was looking for: a gold key with a plastic label hanging from it marked Cell Alarm. She gave it a quarter turn.

SCREEEE—

Della held her breath. Closed her eyes.

No sound but the accelerated beat of her own heart.

She turned and gazed about the room. Her body stiffened, and at first she didn't understand why.

But then she heard it.

The silence was heavy. A pulsating throb, almost too deep to register. But it was there.

Suddenly she missed the squeal of the alarm. She glanced back down the corridor of cells. Fear plucked at her gut strings.

You're being stupid.

No.

It's just a generator or something.

She wanted to believe it. She wanted to accept the easy solution.

But no. Whatever it was that she could hear, or sense - was there really even a sound? - it was alive, somehow. Breathing. An encroaching ugliness that existed all around her.

She had been wrong about Chalkstone. Behind the sleepy facade there was something else, some other monstrous thing, lying dormant, waiting, ready to strike -

This is ridiculous.

Yeah.

Yeah, it was.

She couldn't believe she had let this place get to her.

She stepped around the desk and headed for the exit. Grabbed the plastic keycard on her belt.

Or maybe, she thought, as an image of April flitted through the transom of her mind, *it has already awoken.*

She shuddered. Pressed her card to the plate.

The door unlocked with a *thunk.* She pulled it open.

Next time she'd just leave the stupid alarm ringing.

CHAPTER 8

Della emptied the contents of her locker into her brown suede backpack, and it felt *so* good. She ran through the details of the trip in her mind, the way she had done practically every day since Donna had confirmed the booking. Fly out to Boston, see her parents, stay the weekend. Take the train with Donna through NYC and Philly to DC, stay a few nights, see the sights - for her sins she had never been to the capital - then hire a car for the rest of the journey. Nashville, Memphis, New Orleans, Orlando, Tampa, and finally Miami.

Della didn't have a particularly long or adventurous bucket list - marry, have two kids, live quietly in the suburbs - but seeing her own country was and always had been there at the top, re-scored and underlined. She'd get to the rest of the list eventually.

Sergeant Graham Andrews entered the locker room and they exchanged nods. He was not a man Della knew well - they worked in different departments, they only ever met when their shifts crossed over, and Della had the sneaking suspicion that Sergeant Graham Andrews was not a man that anybody here knew particularly well - but she liked him, and they had exchanged chit-chat on occasion.

There was something intriguing about him; something not quite right. He had a haunted look in his eyes, and that was something Della recognized. She saw it every time she looked in the mirror.

"Off now, newbie?" Graham asked, removing his leather biker jacket.

Della struggled to cram everything into her backpack. How long would she need to be here before people stopped calling her *newbie?* Until there was a new newbie, she guessed. But it rankled with her. The word had the connotation of *rookie,* and she was such a very long way from that.

She'd suffered it all before, of course, most recently when she'd joined the Special Investigations Unit in Cambridge, Massachusetts. More than a decade learning the ropes as a beat cop in Boston and she still had detectives several years her junior treating her like she was wet behind the ears. One of the consequences of being a young-looking woman, she supposed. As with all good things in life, there had to be a downside. But Graham, she knew, didn't mean anything by it. Besides, in his Suffolk accent the word came out sounding like 'nooby', and it really was quite sweet.

"Got a plane to catch," she said. "Going home."

Graham took a pair of epaulettes from his locker and buttoned them to his shirt. "Good for you. I bet you're keen to get out of this madhouse for a while, huh?"

She wasn't sure how to respond to that. Being a foreigner, she didn't want to offend him with her opinion of Chalkstone. It was a very quiet town, and she'd not exactly been rushed off her feet since she'd been here. Which was fine; that had been precisely her reason for transferring in the first place. But given what she had just experienced downstairs, she was keen to get out of this town as quickly as possible, and a little knot formed in her belly at the thought of ever having to return.

"Yeah," she said with a chuckle. Keep it light, she figured. "Just handed off a strange case, actually."

"Oh?" He slid his body armor over his head and hung the leather jacket in his locker.

"Babysitter died falling down the stairs. She was high, you know..."

Della mimed toking on a joint. Graham looked at her, the deeply etched lines on his forehead creasing, but he didn't respond.

Della felt a bit silly. "Anyway, she really spooked the kid with this creepy little children's book, and now the kid thinks the book did it."

"Did what?"

"Killed the babysitter."

Graham's eyes widened. Della felt embarrassed and a little ashamed. She glanced away, stuffing the last of her belongings into her bag. "I know, I know. But she honestly believes it was the book."

"What was it called?"

"Huh?"

"The book."

"Oh, I, I don't remember. But it was this gruesome, twisted fairytale. *Curious* something. She reckons it scared the babysitter to death."

She tied up the backpack and snapped the clasp. Heaved it onto her shoulder. Looked back at Graham.

She froze.

He stood there, mouth agape, staring back at her. His motorcycle helmet hung loosely at his side.

She watched him for a moment. "Are you alright?"

He didn't respond. He had glazed over.

She moved toward him, but his eyes didn't follow. "Graham? Graham?"

He snapped out of it, his eyes fixing her with a stern glare. "Describe the book."

He had thrown her. She didn't know what to say. She fumbled for an answer, struggling to remember specific details.

"It was old. Almost falling apart. It had a leather cover decorated with a picture of a little girl. She... well, she had an apple tree growing out of her ears."

Graham's motorcycle helmet dropped to the floor with a clang. He made no effort to retrieve it.

"Graham?"

His face had turned a leaden gray. He stumbled backward and fell onto the bench.

Della dashed over. "Graham, are you okay?"

"Bring the girl in," he said, without looking up.

"Don't worry, it's taken care of. I've already made arrangements. Silas is dealing with it. She's coming in for a video interview next week."

"No!" He clamped a large hand on her shoulder.

She flinched. "I don't understand..."

His eyes burned into her. "It'll be too late by then. Bring the girl in. Bring her in now."

CHAPTER 9

The room set aside for interviewing children was very much the same as an ordinary interview room. A cold, bare cell with crumbling brick walls painted a sour yellow. Except this room had a ripped and faded poster of Barney the Dinosaur on the wall above the table.

Nice to see they made an effort, Della thought, as she stashed her bulging backpack between her feet. She checked her watch. She still had time; the flight didn't leave for another three hours.

April yawned. The poor girl probably hadn't slept, and now she'd been dragged in here directly after breakfast. She held on tight to the arm of her mother, a woman who looked like she'd slept in her make-up and been hurriedly awoken with a hangover.

"Thanks for coming in at such short notice," Della said. "This really shouldn't take long."

"Your accent's funny," April said.

Della chuckled. "I'm American."

"Where Disneyland is?"

"That's right."

"I'd like to go to America sometime."

"Me too," Della sighed.

Graham entered and slammed the door. He marched over to the table and took a seat beside Della. He had always struck her as such an easy-going kind of guy. To see him looking so rattled... It disturbed her.

She offered him a pen. "You want to write the statement?"

He continued to stare ahead, studying April.

Della took the pen back. "Okay, I'll do it then, shall I?"

He didn't respond.

She asked the girl her name for the record, and began writing. *I am April Willis. I made this statement in the presence of my mother.*

"What can you tell me about the book?" Graham began. "How did you get it?"

April cowered under his glare. "I...I don't know. I'd never seen it before."

Her mother spoke. "We recently cleared out the attic. There was this dusty old box of books. Mostly encyclopedias and travel guides, a few children's books. It must have been one of those."

Graham nodded. "I see."

Della stopped writing and looked up. She noticed he was sweating profusely.

Graham cleared his throat. "Now. Your babysitter -" He turned to Della.

"Elizabeth Paul," Della said. *Good to know I'm needed for something.*

"Right, right." He turned back to April. "Elizabeth read to you from this book?"

"For a little bit. But then she stopped. She got scared."

"What frightened her? Do you know?"

"Take your time," Della said, and April smiled. Graham huffed and checked his watch.

"She didn't want to open the book again. She started crying and said a bad word. I told her she was naughty, Mommy."

"Good girl," her mother said, patting her on the back of the hand.

"Why was she so upset?" Graham asked. "Why didn't she want to open the book?"

"There was something scratched into the cover. A message. It made her freak out. The words..." She trailed off, looking embarrassed.

"It's okay," Della said.

"They weren't there at first," April continued. "And then...they were."

Graham leaned forward. "They just appeared?"

"The first time, yes. But the second time..."

Della gritted her teeth. She didn't like where this was going. She knew Graham would have no patience for a pre-teen's overactive imagination.

"The second time, I saw it for myself. I saw the words scratch onto the book. As if they were being written by the Invisible Man."

"April," Della said, "I know it's difficult, but please try and stick to the facts as best you can. Tell us only what really happened."

April shot her a wounded look. "But that is what really happened."

Graham put a hand on Della's arm. "It's okay." He turned back to April. "What were the words?"

April hesitated. She looked over at Della, who smiled reassuringly.

"What did they say?" Graham barked.

April flinched.

"Take it easy," Della whispered to Graham.

He didn't listen. "April. Tell me."

The girl released a great, shuddering sigh. "They were angry."

"Angry?"

"Lizzie couldn't even look at them. It was like the book was shouting." She turned to her mother. "I want to go home, Mommy."

Graham sprung to his feet, placing his hands on the table. "Was it a warning? What did it say?"

Della leaned in. "Sergeant…"

His eyes were fixed on April.

The girl glossed over for a moment.

Graham clicked his fingers, and April jumped. She was back in the room. She glanced up at him, her eyes welling with tears. "It said..." Her bottom lip trembled. A tear trickled down her cheek. "It said, 'Don't look inside'."

Graham took a sharp intake of breath. A vein pulsed on the side of his head. Sweat trickled into his eyes.

His hands gripped tight to the edge of the table, causing it to wobble, and his knuckles to whiten. His eyebrows knotted.

A long moment of silence.

April's mom turned to Della and whispered. "Is he alright?"

Della reached up and put a hand on Graham's shoulder. His shirt was soaking wet, and stuck to his back. He was perfectly still. It appeared that he had stopped breathing altogether.

A muscle twitched in his forearm.

Without warning a torrent of vomit exploded from his mouth and gushed over the surface of the table.

April recoiled. Her mother leapt to her feet. Her chair crashed to the floor behind her.

"Oh dear," Della said, jumping up. "Oh my goodness." She grabbed a wad of paper towels from a dispenser. "I'm very sorry about this."

Graham wiped his mouth with his sleeve and snatched the towels from her. "I've got it."

Vomit hung from the table in fat drips and puddled onto the checkered floor tiles below. The smell hit Della's nose and she gagged. She poured a cup of water from the cooler and offered it to Graham.

He waved it away. He placed paper towels over the surface of the table. They soaked through instantly. He bunched up a handful of fresh towels and got down on his knees, scrubbing furiously at the tiles.

Della ushered April and her mother to the door. She noticed little spots of Graham's puke on the little girl's dress. "I'm so sorry about this. Thank you, thank you very much, we really appreciate you coming in, you've been very helpful…"

Graham halted his clean-up. "Wait!"

Everybody froze.

"Where is it? The book?"

"It's gone," April's mother said. "Don't worry."

Graham clambered to his feet. Vomit stains decorated the knees of his black trousers. "Where?"

She looked down at the floor. "April couldn't sleep with it in the house. So my husband boxed it up with all the other old books and put it out in the yard. He got rid of it this morning."

Graham threw down a wad of drenched paper towels. They hit the floor with a thick splat.

"Where?" he growled. "Tell me. Where is the book now?"

CHAPTER 10

Morag Mountjoy sighed and lifted another sealed cardboard box onto the counter. This one was heavier than it looked. She stood there a moment, her fist pressed against the small of her back, wincing. Once the pain had passed she slashed through the tape with her box cutter, pulled open the flaps and peered inside.

Of the myriad little tasks that made up her job, this was her least favorite, each box she opened feeling like a fresh dagger to her heart. Chalkstone Public Library had always been more than just a workplace to her; it had been her sanctuary for the past several decades, somewhere *peaceful* in a world gone to the dogs, and, of course, it had introduced her to the love of her life - reading. Sure, the library had fallen into disrepair over the years, but it was still a grand and beautiful building, and it deserved good books.

Donations, she had always insisted, were not the way to go. She had fought hard against the idea, even refusing to draw up the *Give Generously* posters when dotty Deirdre Ackerman had requested her assistance, but that was before the council halved their funding, and before the building renovations emptied the pot, and now she found herself, once a week, trudging through cardboard boxes full of tatty cast-offs with as much disdain as she could muster.

She considered it her job to separate the wheat from the chaff - she couldn't stand to have the stacks of her beloved library stuffed with trash - but it was a straightforward enough job, given that Morag rarely found anything shelf-worthy. A large percentage of the books she received were defaced in some way, often scribbled on, or water damaged, or soiled with unspeakable bodily fluids, and occasionally the content itself was inappropriate - she'd thrown away a lot of erotica.

She rummaged through the large box, pulled out a few brochures and old newspapers, and dumped them on the reject pile. A couple of travel books looked passable until she leafed through them and the pages fell out. Two random volumes of an encyclopedia - in this case, the letters F and U (she found this ironically appropriate) - were useless without the rest of the set. Next, she pulled out a leather-bound book with a striking apple tree illustration on the cover.

Now wait a minute...

She examined the book closely. This had potential. It was clearly very old, and worn at the corners. There were some scratches in the leather...

A young girl giggled loudly in Junior Fiction. Morag tutted. She craned her neck, looking over her glasses, and gave the pigtailed culprit a stern look. She put her finger to her mouth and *ssh*-ed her. The girl looked away sheepishly.

Morag shook her head. Libraries used to be a place for grown-ups. Now they were just one more hang-out for noisy brats.

She returned her attention to the book. A smile flirted with her lips. This was something special, she could tell by the simplest of touches: the embossed detail of individual leaves on the cover, the lime green silk of the ribbon marker tucked within the gilded gold that edged its pages. It was in far from mint condition, but this was, nevertheless, a handsome tome. She flicked through it, inhaling its musty aroma, the smell summoning foggy memories of her first school, and learning to read in the attic room with the delightful Miss Moore.

She admired the fine work of the many detailed illustrations, including one in which a hard-faced child stuck her tongue out in the shadow of her disapproving mother. It was a beautifully bound and heavy book, the pages discolored but thick with quality. She closed it and perused the spine. Typed the title and author into the catalogue search box on her computer. The database brought back no results, and at long last that smile surfaced.

One for the keep pile.

She pasted a slip on the inside front cover, placing it precisely and symmetrically beneath the vine-leaf vignette. She scanned the barcode on the slip. She gave the book a call number and entered its details on the system. She set it carefully aside, a small sigh of satisfaction emanating from the corner of her thin mouth. She pulled another book from the box.

Something moved at the edge of her vision. On the countertop.

She froze. *What…?*

Before she could even ask the question in her mind, she already knew the answer.

Samuel Whiskers.

It was back. She hadn't seen it in over a fortnight, the rat that stalked the stacks; she hoped it had succumbed to one of her traps, but she had a sneaking suspicion that dotty Deirdre Ackerman was protecting it, maybe even keeping it as a pet in her office, for it was she who had named it, after her favorite Beatrix Potter character. The crazy bitch was probably, Morag imagined, sitting at her desk right now knitting little outfits for it.

Morag kept perfectly still and moved only her eyes. She didn't want to spook the little bastard. But what she saw as her eyes darted over to the corner of the counter was not a rat.

Her heart lurched. The cover of the book with the embossed illustration was *moving*. The surface rippled, as if made not of leather but some thick, oily liquid.

It's melting, her mind gasped, and she tutted at her own foolishness.

Of course. The cover is made of that rare and magical leather, sourced from the hides of the famous sun-shy melting cattle.

She leaned forward and pushed her glasses over the bridge of her nose for a closer look. What she observed defied belief, and would have sent a more feeble-minded woman - *hello, Deirdre Ackerman* - sailing clean off her rocker. But Morag was of stern Scottish stock, and she wasn't going to let a bizarre little thing like this relieve her of her sanity.

Now that she was nearer she could see that the cover was not melting, but that its many intricate parts were animated somehow. Tiny blades of leather grass shimmered in the light of an unseen sun. Raised leaves fluttered in an imaginary breeze. The branches of the apple tree swayed and bowed under the weight of the plump apples bobbing at their tips. The little girl from whose ears the branches grew was being tugged, first one way then the other, her long hair tangled in the bark, her head seesawing from side to side, her eyebrows lifting and falling, lifting and falling. But the emotion expressed in her pinched features was not alarm; it was joy.

As Morag watched, a leafy, rope-like vine wrapped itself around the girl's neck and pulled tight, digging deep into her flesh. The more it tightened, the wider the child's mouth became, her lips pulling back to form a hideous grin, revealing a clumsy keyboard of rotted teeth. Her moldy green eyes bulged from their sockets, unblinking.

If Morag didn't know any better, she would have thought the girl's eyes were fixed on *her*.

She fell into a lazy trance as she watched, unable to tear herself away from the tottering demon girl, whose mouth creased ever-upward into a grin of such immense proportions that it threatened to pop the round apples of her cheeks.

The leather suddenly and noisily ripped, halting all movement and breaking Morag from her daze. She looked on, dismay spreading across her features as a hole gouged into the cover between the now still branches and pulled down, creating a furrow line so deep that it had surely buried itself into the pages beyond.

Morag's jaw dropped. A crescent shape etched into the leather, from the peak of the ripped line and round, creating a *D*. Then beside that, a perfect circle for an *O*.

She snapped her head up, certain now that someone was standing over her, scratching into the book with a sharp implement.

She stepped back, as if giving this invisible vandal room to work, and watched, helplessly, as the cover continued to be defaced.

DON'T

She glanced around the library. Everyone was going about their business as usual. Skinny Phillip Flatt was attending to a long line of lenders at the check-out desk. A gaggle of schoolgirls sat huddled at one of the study tables, sharing muffled gossip behind their manicured hands. Several browsers perused books in the Reference section, no doubt undoing much of the work Morag had recently done to tidy the shelves. In Junior Fiction, a young mother was helping her son with his choice of pop-up book.

Morag's eyes dropped back to the cover.

DON'T
LOOK
INSIDE

Her mouth formed into the shape of a scream, but being a well-trained librarian, no sound escaped her lips. Her hands bolted out, shoving the book over the counter. She heard it clatter to the floor.

Her legs gave way and she stumbled back, losing a shoe. She fell onto her chair, which skated back a few inches on its castors until it thumped against a filing cabinet.

She stared numbly ahead, her fingers trembling as she gripped tightly to the hem of her skirt. She gazed into the contents of the open stationery drawer beneath the counter. Questions attempted to form in her frazzled mind, questions beginning with *what...* and *why...* and *how...*

She was seriously low on staples, she noticed. And the ones in her stapler were an irregular size, which was a pain because it meant they had to be specially ordered from a separate supplier.

Why don't I just order in a stapler that uses regular sized staples?

Of course. That made much more sense. Odd that she'd never thought to do that until now...

The demon girl's expanding grin flashed through her mind. She blinked it away.

What would happen, she suddenly thought, *if I looked inside?*

A little boy giggled nearby. His mother called after him in hushed tones. "Freddy! Freddy, come back here!"

What would happen, Morag thought with rising dread, *if someone else were to look inside?*

She saw the flash of a red coat as the boy passed between the tower of boxes and the counter. She panicked.

It's okay, her mind reasoned. *It would never interest him. Kids like bright and cheerful books.*

"What have you got there?" Freddy's mother said.

His response turned Morag's blood cold.

"It's a scary book, mommy."

CHAPTER 11

Do something.

Morag wanted to leap to her feet, to dash around the counter and grab the book from the little boy's grasp.

But she didn't. Those three horrible words flashed through her mind, keeping her glued to the chair.

Another burst of red flickered past her vision as the boy returned to his mother. Part of her was glad, she realized with a sudden wave of guilt, that the book was now farther away.

A pulsing thundered in her temples. She closed her eyes and tried to listen.

"Okay, sit here. Let's have a look, then." The mother's voice.

"Look, Mommy. An apple tree."

"Oh yes. It's a very pretty cover, isn't it?"

Surely…? Morag's eyes snapped open. *Surely they can see the warning?*

She raised herself from the seat of the chair, stretching her neck, peering over the countertop. The boy sat at one of the tables in Junior Fiction. His mother knelt down beside him. She opened the book to a random page.

Morag held her breath.

"Okay, are you ready?" The woman began to read.

Cat was a curious little girl
With a pinafore dress and a cutesy curl.
Always hungry, she loved to eat
Juicy apples were her favorite treat.

"Don't swallow the pips," her mother said,
"Or an apple tree will grow out of your head."
Cat was curious; what splendid fun!
She bought twenty apples and ate every one.

She waited, but nothing; and then, close to tears
Two leafy tree branches grew out of her ears.
Soon the branches bore fruit, and Cat could see
That she'd always have plenty of apples for tea.

"That was good, wasn't it?" the woman said.

"Nah, I like this one." The boy waved a colorful board book in the air.

"Why don't we borrow that, then? Come on."

Morag watched as they left, the little boy running ahead of his mother. The book remained behind, still open on the table. Her leg twitched, as if her body wanted to go and retrieve the book, but a commanding voice barked an order in her mind.

Stay.

A cold shiver ran down Morag's arms, sprinkling goosebumps across her flesh. The voice in her head was that of Mrs Lanscombe, the lady who ran the dog obedience classes at Chalkstone Kennels. A voice Morag had long forgotten, or so she thought.

Stay.

Morag had taken her two-year-old, Puck. He was excitable, as young dogs always were, but he bounded around like a crazy thing at the slightest provocation and she had worried that he'd get himself hurt one of these days. So she had taken him to Mrs Lanscombe's classes, and the change in him had been evident immediately. The woman seemed to have a magical way around animals. Something about the firm but serene tone of her voice had all the dogs in the class enraptured, like good little schoolchildren, and they all wanted to please her, especially Puck. Even Mrs Lanscombe said that he was her star pupil.

Morag had taken to mimicking the woman's commands around the house, eventually developing a half-decent imitation of her, and Puck had responded well. That was, until one day a couple of months later, when, waiting by the side of the road, Morag delivered her best Mrs Lanscombe *stay*, but Puck didn't stay, and instead he stepped merrily out into traffic, and his long snout was snapped sideways by a Land Rover. He didn't die straight away, either. He bounced back onto his paws and scampered about until the impact of a second vehicle broke his back, and then he collapsed and died in the road with his face hanging off.

Stay.

Morag watched the book from the safety of her little den behind the counter, unable to peel her eyes away. The book's unique and terrible magic held a hideous allure. She itched to get over there and look inside. It had spoken to her, the book, but not, it appeared, to the boy and his mother, and as a result she felt a twisted sense of ownership.

Stay.

She slipped her stray shoe onto her foot and shifted around the counter, certain now of what she had to do. She stepped forward and hesitated as her foot hovered over the gripper where the carpet met the linoleum that made up the main floor of the library. In her mind's eye she saw Puck stepping out ahead of her, bounding mindlessly into the rush of traffic. She heard the sickening crunch as his snout snapped.

What am I doing?

And yet she continued on, her flat, sensible shoes making a soft *shlick shlack* across the speckled beige linoleum, her heart drumming in her chest.

The open pages of the book loomed into view, calming her with their plain and unthreatening normality. An illustration on one side, words formed into verses on the other.

Shlick shlack, shlick shlack.

She pulled out the orange plastic chair and dropped into its child-sized seat, her knees so close to the ground that she was unable to fold her legs comfortably beneath her.

She picked up the book and closed it carefully, bracing herself. To her astonishment there were no longer any words carved into the cover; just the embossed apple tree illustration, and it was not animated this time. Even the little girl looked normal - well, as normal as a girl with branches growing from her ears could look.

Confused, Morag flipped the book over and checked the back cover, just in case. Nothing but more intertwined, raised branches loaded with green leather apples.

Did I imagine it?

Was that even possible? She was a nuts and bolts, no-nonsense woman, not prone to hallucinations or waking dreams, nor currently under the influence of any medications or mind altering substances...

She felt a scratching beneath the soft skin of her palm on the other side of the book. Her thumb dipped into a sudden hollow in the cover. She turned the book over and there, carved deep and obscuring much of the illustration, were two words.

DON'T
LOOK

She gasped and shrank back. A third word began beneath the others, the letters slashing furiously into the cover, the leather popping and tearing until, after only a second or two, the warning was complete.

INSIDE

Her breathing was shallow, her throat dry. But mixed in with the fear she felt a strange sensation of relief.

I'm not crazy.

Or was she? Did the re-emergence of the words prove that she was sane, or merely confirm her insanity? If she were to show the words to any of the patrons of the library, would they see only the cover illustration?

Her fingers curled around the edge of the book, poised to open it.

Heed the warning.

Was this really what she wanted? It wasn't too late. She could get up and leave, right now. She could call from home and explain to Deirdre that she'd come down with the flu or something. Maybe watch a couple of episodes of *Quincy* or that other one, the one with Dick Van Dyke - *what was it called?* - to take her mind off this whole silly business. A couple of hours of distraction and soon she would be free of the book's inexplicable draw.

Torn shreds of leather flapped around the letters as she lifted the cover. The words had burrowed so deep that they were now etched clearly into the inside front page, pulping the slip Morag had pasted there only minutes earlier.

DON'T
LOOK
INSIDE

A second chance. Time to rethink. What was the sensible course of action here? She ran her fingers over the grooves in the paper. She followed the shape of the *D*, the *O*, the *N* and the *T*...

She smarted as a sharp edge snagged and dug into her flesh. She yanked her hand away, leaving behind a small blob of crimson.

Blast it. She put her finger to her mouth and sucked the wound.

Diagnosis: Murder. That was it! How could she forget? She loved that show.

She glanced up. A flash of white disappeared behind the stacks in Nonfiction. She watched, following the shape. She saw the outline of a figure between the gaps in the shelves.

Sheila O'Hare.

She was back. It had been a while - in fact, Morag thought she remembered reading somewhere that the crazy bitch had finally been sectioned. But maybe she dreamt it, because here she was, wearing her nightgown as usual. *Better get out the air freshener*, Morag thought. Sheila always left a stink of stale urine in her wake.

Morag flipped past what remained of the inside front page. The book had an unpleasant smell to it now; a dry, dust-rot smell that wrinkled her nose and made her think of dark, creepy attics and cobwebs and rat droppings. The next page was blank, save for a two-word dedication:

For Morag.

She snorted nervous laughter, amused by what she hoped was a mere coincidence. She turned the page carefully, worried that the paper might cut her again, and as she did so her face dropped.

The dedication, she realized, had been no coincidence. The contents of this book were for her eyes only. The first thing she saw on the fresh page had confirmed this, beyond all question of doubt.

Morag Mountjoy.

The first two words on the opening line of the first verse. She couldn't bring herself to read on;

not yet. She felt a sudden and powerful wave of nausea.

She glanced to the opposite page, distracted by the illustration of a handsome trinket box with a keyhole in its hinged lid. The box was made of what looked, to Morag, like polished rosewood. She had owned a similar box, once.

Sheila O'Hare was sectioned, Morag thought. *I read it in the Evening News only last month.*

Her head shot up, her vision trained on the stacks where she had last spotted Sheila. There was still somebody there, an outline in a white nightgown.

Morag's stomach rolled. She knew it wasn't Sheila. That was clear now. The hair was matted and red, not Sheila's silvery gray, and the frame was much slighter -

The figure inexplicably shifted, disappearing and reappearing within the blink of an eye, a few yards farther down the aisle. Closer to Morag's position.

Morag's fingers tightened around the book. She watched, unblinking, as a head rose up between the shelves, black eyes peering over the books, fixed on her.

She gasped and looked away, unable to meet the thing's gaze. For it was a thing, she now decided, and not a woman. She cringed, a whimper escaping her lips. She steeled herself and looked back.

It was gone.

Her eyes darted about. She waited for it to reappear, fully expecting it to materialize next to her. She clutched at her chest even before she felt the sharp stabbing in her heart. She knew the pain would pass soon, as it always did, but she had an immediate and terrifying feeling that she was going to die today.

Don't be ridiculous, you daft old bat.

The pain receded. It was still there, tugging at her insides, but she chose to ignore it. She was a strong woman; she'd survived tougher times than this. She sat up and straightened her cardigan.

I'll be fine. She cleared her throat. Allowed the murmuring quiet of the library to wash over her. *My favorite place in the whole world,* she reminded herself. *My home from home.* She took a few lungfuls of air, pushed her glasses high onto the bridge of her nose and returned her attention to the book.

The words shifted into focus. She began to read.

> *Morag Mountjoy never told a soul*
> *But her vile little secret took its toll.*
> *A truth that threatened to drive her insane*
> *Until she locked it deep inside her brain.*
>
> *Now we're here to open the box*
> *To turn the key and flip the locks.*
> *To lift the lid and peer inside*
> *For forty years, what did you hide?*

Those last words hit home and Morag's head swam. *It can't be...*

There was only one thing in this world that Morag knew, deep down, could defeat her. One thing that she was not strong enough to survive.

And the book knew exactly what it was.

CHAPTER 12

Morag did the math and it had indeed been forty years, although it seemed even longer. It was such a distant memory that any length of time attributed to it would, in her mind, feel wrong. Her recall of the event was abstract at best. But that had been intentional, of course. Had she not severed herself emotionally from that period of her life then the guilt and remorse and self-hatred would have consumed her long ago. For all the world, though, it felt like it had happened to someone else, as if it was some terrible piece of gossip she had overheard at whist drive.

It struck her what a good job she had done, compartmentalizing almost a year of her life. She really had packed everything away in that polished wooden box.

She closed her eyes. Opened them again.

The *thing* in the nightgown was there.

Morag's mind screamed.

It stood behind the counter, in Morag's den, its head down, bulging eyes blazing from dark sockets, watching her from beneath sharply arched brows. A sunken grin formed in the gray blankness where moments before there had been no mouth. It was an expression Morag recognized instantly. She had seen it only minutes earlier, on the little girl in the cover illustration, as the vine had tightened around her throat.

She leapt to her feet, knocking over the little orange chair. She snatched up the book and scuttled away from Junior Fiction.

Shlick shlack, shlick shlack.

She could feel those eyes on her, but could not look back. She was certain that if she did, that thing's relentless stare would drill its way directly into her soul and obliterate all traces of her sanity.

That ship's sailed, love, a voice in her head piped up. *You really think anything will be normal upstairs after this?*

She made it past Reference and into the study area. The view of her counter was obscured by bookshelves. *Thank heaven for small mercies.*

She drifted along the bank of computer stations and chose a cubicle three in from the end, where she felt less exposed.

She settled down, grateful for the privacy afforded by the side partitions but still able to see much of the library from her seat. She shifted the keyboard to one side, her wrinkled hands trembling uncontrollably. She placed the book on the desktop and turned the page, struggling to get her breath back.

The polished wooden box again. At first she thought the illustration was the same, but then she noticed one small difference: a brass key was now sticking out of the lock.

You worry the truth will be too much to take
That your heart will fail and your mind will break.
It's cruel to keep you in suspense
So let our dazzling show commence.

Her lips mouthed the words as she read, and when she had finished her lips continued on, gibbering with a fear that had consumed her whole body. Her shoes clattered rhythmically against the chair legs. A vein pulsed in her neck.

Thunk. The illustrated key turned in the lock.

Morag wondered if once again she was seeing things. Before she was able to finish the thought the lid of the box popped open, revealing a ballerina figurine in a crumpled tutu, posed forever with her arms raised above her head.

And then it began.

The ballerina slowly rotated. A tinkling music box tune started to play.

Beethoven's *Für Elise.* Tinny, but unmistakable. Morag winced at the noise.

Sshh. She looked around, convinced that others in the library would be able to hear the music. Nobody paid her any attention.

She listened to the tune. A rush of insight brought with it recollections of the box and the ballerina inside, the memory slotting back into her mind like a file missing all these years. Sarah loved that tune. It was the only thing that could ever

(stop the crying)

settle her in the evenings. But there was something else. The scent of lavender drifted through the air, as if carried by the melody. It wrinkled Morag's nose, sparking images in her mind: Sarah, wriggling on the change mat. The tub of baby powder. She had always smothered her in it after bathing her. It was a soothing smell, both for mommy and baby. But it still didn't

(stop the crying)

Cyclops Mountjoy! Yes, of course! A big, blue teddy bear. Originally she'd named him Teddy Mountjoy, but he had button eyes and one of them had fallen off when Sarah was only a week old. Nowadays, such a toy would have been considered unsafe for babies, but Sarah loved ol' Cyclops. Although it was still never enough to

(stop the crying, oh, the incessant crying)

She worried for the baby so much in those first few weeks. Such a delicate little thing. On countless occasions Morag had fallen asleep on the floor beside the crib because she was terrified that Sarah might stop breathing if she left the room, or that the multi-colored blanket Morag had knitted, from a pattern given to her by her sister, might ride up and smother poor baby while she slept. But it never did, of course. And Sarah loved that blanket so. Not that it was ever enough to

(stop the crying oh god why won't it stop just shut the hell up just stop just stop just stop)

Ah, the music box. What a blessing that was! An extra bottle or a cuddle rarely did the job, but opening the music box was a reliable soother. Sarah never paid attention to the ballerina, but that tune always did the trick.

Always.

Until one day, that fateful day, it had failed to

(stop the crying what's wrong with her she won't stop there must be something wrong no stop just stop please make it stop please stop please no)

It had been an incredibly hot Friday in July. Not even particularly sunny, just humid. Morag was sweating and miserable and itchy and desperately tired. She had restless legs and the heat was unbearable...

On this day, of all days, the tinkling melody just wasn't enough. Maybe Sarah felt the heat, maybe she didn't. Her room was cool. But the trusty music box, on which Morag had learned to depend, spectacularly failed to

(stop the crying just shut up just shut up why won't you shut up shut up JUST SHUT UP SHUT UP SHUT UP SHUT THE FUCK UP)

Morag jolted in her chair, her mind thrust back into the present. She was out of breath.

The music box wound down, playing its last, slow notes as the ballerina performed her final revolution.

Turning to a stop, the ballerina's face appeared, her delicate painted features contorting, her pretty eyes narrowing into dark slits, her perfect bow lips stretching wide to form a demonic grin.

Morag flinched. She looked away. Down at the book. The words on the page drew her in.

'Ssh,' you tell the kids browsing books
If they're noisy you give them disdainful looks.
But there was once a child who wouldn't obey
So you had to shut her up in another way.

Please, no… Morag dragged her hands down her face, unable to shake the horror.

"I didn't mean it," she whispered. "It was an accident. A terrible accident."

Her heart was beating too hard in her chest. She had to do something. She reached for the book, meaning to close it for the final time, but instead her fingers grabbed the corner of the page, as if drawn there by a powerful magnetic force.

She watched helplessly as a fresh page revealed itself.

They called it crib death; we know it's not true
Your punishment is long overdue.
You seem sweet, harmless, meek and mild
Who would have guessed you killed a child?

The illustration on the facing page depicted a woman sitting at what looked like one of the computer stations at Chalkstone Public Library. The angle of the drawing was from behind the woman. Morag recognized the woolen cardigan, the narrow shoulders, and the way the figure was hunched over the desk.

She had never seen the back of her own head, but that was unmistakably what she saw on the page. She felt a desperate urge to turn around, thinking that if she did she might witness the illustrator drawing the very image she currently held in her hands.

Her eye was drawn to something else in the picture. On the computer monitor. At first it seemed like a blur of black and white shapes, but soon she realized it was a face, and the face was grinning.

She looked up from the book and gazed directly into the computer screen perched in front of her. She saw her own reflection. She exhaled.

Something appeared behind her in the monitor. Something dressed in white. The figure leaned in, over Morag's shoulder, its sneering face filling the screen.

Morag felt something brush past her neck. She gasped in horror. She scooped the book up and shrank away, ducking out of her seat. Fear bolted down her spine as she scurried past the bank of computers and back onto the linoleum floor.

The thing was behind her now, and she intended to keep it that way. She could see the exit doors in the distance, on the front wall of the library beyond the check-out desk. There were ten, maybe twelve stacks between her and the desk.

Shlick shlack, shlick shlack.

Faster now.

She felt those evil eyes on her. The library had never looked so long. It stretched out before her, the exit seemingly not drawing any closer, even as she picked up her pace.

She couldn't bring herself to look back. She glanced to her left and gazed down the stacks as she passed.

The thing stood at the bottom of the aisle.

Watching her.

She jolted, dropping the book. It clattered to the floor.

Pick it up, her mind yelled.

No time.

What if someone were to read it? I'd be locked up until the end of my days.

That thought slowed her down. She saw herself, in her mind's eye, turning around and going back for the book. But she didn't. She couldn't.

The thing was back there. And also, it appeared, to the side of her. But especially back there. It *owned* back there. That was *its* territory.

The only way was forward. She had to get out of this place. Chalkstone Public Library, the building that had once been her sanctuary, was going to be the scene of her death if she didn't get out of there fast.

Gasping for breath, she picked up her pace again. She passed the next aisle. Glanced down the stacks.

Incredibly, there it was again. In the same place at the bottom of the aisle, its eyes trained on her.

She screamed.

She passed a little girl with pigtails. The same girl she had reprimanded earlier. The girl put her finger to her lips and *ssh*-ed her.

Morag ran as fast as she could. An alien feeling spread down her side. She remembered it as a stitch. It had been many years since life had necessitated anything more than walking speed.

The next aisle approached. *I won't look.*

But she couldn't help herself. She glanced down the stacks.

She saw its white nightgown in a blur.

She lost her shoe.

Can't go back.

She limped on. Looking ahead now. She was close.

Shlack. Shlack. Shlack.

Soon she would pass the line of lenders at the check-out desk. She couldn't see skinny Phillip Flatt through the gaggle of them, but she knew he was there, and soon he would see her. He would clock her haunted expression. He would wonder why on earth she was running. He would come out to help, and he would slow her down. But it would be a friendly face, at least. She liked Phillip. She might even feel safe with Phillip.

She could see behind the desk now.

To her horror, she discovered it wasn't Phillip standing there.

She stopped, skidding a little, her one shoe screeching on the linoleum.

The thing stared back at her from behind the check-out desk.

The exit doors swept open, beckoning her, but she couldn't come. Her vision swam, the library ceiling tilting down, the checkered floor bending up toward her.

She darted into the final aisle and headed down the stack, running her fingers along the books as she went.

Spiritualism. Her favorite section.

She had a strange feeling that the books might protect her, somehow. She had looked after them all these years; fixed them up when they were falling apart, sorted them according to subject matter, tidied their shelves. Now it was time for the books to return the favor.

She reached the end of the aisle and collapsed to her knees, sobbing between gulps of air. Her body ached and her head throbbed.

Something blotted out the light.

She turned her head slowly, fear rising above the pain.

A figure stood there, silhouetted against the light from the main floor. In one swift movement it reached down and picked her up under her arms. It held her aloft, her feet dangling inches from the carpet.

Like lifting a baby from a crib.

Its vice-like fingers gripped tight, bruising her skin. Her remaining shoe clattered to the floor.

She stared down into its face.

The mouth was not grinning now, but grimacing. Blood seeped through split lips. Its eyes blazed with fury. The gray skin, a mosaic of cracks, rotted around the cheekbones.

It was not a thing, she could see that now. It was - or at least had once been - a woman.

The thing that had once been a woman shook her violently.

In the agony of her dying moments, Morag looked into its eyes and in a flash of perfect clarity she *understood.*

Its lips parted and a sound escaped. It seemed to speak, but its voice did not belong. *"Stop it,"* the thing said. *"Stop it. Just stop it, just stop it, just stop it."*

Morag recognized the voice. It was her own.

"Please," the monster begged. *"Just stop crying."*

All was dark now. Morag felt no pain. She was vaguely aware that she was still suspended in the air. Still in its grip. Still being shaken.

With her last breath and all of her remaining energy, she opened her mouth and whispered.

"Thank you."

CHAPTER 13

Cat's Curiosity by Bertrand Powell lay in an undignified heap on the linoleum floor, its cover splayed open, its pages collecting the dirt and grime of a thousand pairs of shoes. Another pair settled beside the book, these ones pink, glossy and decorated with shimmering butterflies. The dream shoes of every five-year-old girl. Only this pair were adult-sized.

A dainty hand reached down, its nails sparkling with glittery bubblegum varnish, and caressed the embossed apple tree illustration on the cover.

"Oh, this is to die for!" Rhiannon exclaimed. She knelt beside the book, her shiny pink dress flowing around her ankles. She picked up the book and turned the pages, settling on one of the illustrations. A sweet little girl in a pinafore dress danced merrily in a meadow of daisies.

"Perfect!" She closed the book and held it up to Vince, whose heavily tattooed arms carried a tall pile of books. He bent his knees and received the book on the top of the pile.

The earbuds pressed into Vince's ears currently blasted his favorite death metal band deep into his brain. As a result, he failed to hear the rip and pop as the leather tore open. Nor did he notice, his vacant stare gazing somewhere far away, his mind occupied with thoughts of his busy day ahead, as letters gouged deep into the cover. He followed his girlfriend along to the next aisle.

"And this one," Rhiannon said.

Vince bent his knees again. The new book went on top, obscuring the words of warning now scratched deep into the cover beneath.

CHAPTER 14

Della thought she was going to die.

She held tight to the grip handle on the inside of the car door as Graham raced through morning traffic. His driving skills maintained the expert fluidity of a trained police driver, but something about the way he stared intently ahead, unblinking - it frightened her.

She watched as rows of Victorian terraced houses whizzed past in a blur. She had not yet taken a response driving course, but she knew that it was irresponsible to drive at this speed in a built-up area, no matter how skilled Graham was.

The patrol car swerved sharply around a line of parked vehicles, tossing Della to one side. She stiffened her neck to brace her head. It made her think of the Tilt-A-Whirl she had endured once at a county fair in Boston, and she felt an odd pang of homesickness. She didn't know why; she'd hated that ride. Donna and her mom had thought it was fun, though. They'd wanted to go again, but Della had not, the relentless whirl of the car on its circular track and the blur of tilted lights and faces making her feel sick, just as this car ride made her feel sick. And much like this car ride, she'd had no choice but to suffer through until it was over.

She considered ordering Graham to slow down, but a quick glance at her watch forced a rethink. Time was running out if she was going to make it to the airport.

They approached a line of stationary traffic. Graham flipped a switch on the dash and the siren blared. He edged out into the center of the road. Cars parted before him.

The scream of the siren felt like it was vibrating Della's brain. "Is that really necessary?"

He didn't respond.

She looked over at him. She saw flecks of dried vomit on his shirt collar. "You want to tell me what all that was about back there?"

"Bad bagel," he growled.

A bright orange pine tree swung wildly from the rearview mirror, its pungent *Citrus Zest* stench mixing with the musty smell that pervaded the patrol car to create a sickly new odor, one that was many times more offensive to Della's delicate olfactory senses.

"You know," she said, her backpack bouncing around between her legs, "you were very harsh with that poor girl. She'd been through a terrible trauma."

His eyes flickered over to her. "It was your fault."

She was speechless for a moment. The *gall* of the man. "What?"

"You let the book go."

She glared at him in disbelief. "Let it go? What did you want me to do, throw the cuffs on it?"

They said nothing to each other for several minutes. She supposed it was foolish to think that she could get the measure of someone based on a few brief conversations in the locker room, but still, it shocked her, how little she really knew this guy.

Graham broke the silence. He spoke softer this time. "It's dangerous."

She could barely hear him over the roar of the engine and the squeal of the siren. "What?"

"The book. It's dangerous."

She felt a plummeting feeling in her stomach. Her life was in the hands of a crazy person. "What do you mean? It's a book, okay? Just a book."

"Hah!"

Della waited for more, but nothing was forthcoming. "Hello? You wanna let me in on the secret here?"

He sighed. "It's a long story."

She wanted to scream. In her mind, she pictured herself shaking him. Slapping him about the face.

In reality, she tutted. "Seriously, Graham. This is my case. And despite all evidence to the contrary, you're the one along for the ride, okay? I'm allowing you in. So you need to give me something."

He eyeballed her. "What were you running away from?"

"Excuse me?"

"When you moved here. To England. What was it that you couldn't cope with back home?"

Della studied him. Avoidance. Deflection. He was more like a criminal than a cop. Or maybe that's what being on the job for so many years did to a person. Either way, she knew she would get nothing from him. For now.

The car pulled into the grounds of the library. Graham slammed on the brakes, dumping the vehicle across two parking spaces. He leapt out.

"Hey, wait!" Della climbed out of the car and chased after him.

The entrance doors parted as Graham stepped inside. They began to close as Della approached. The doors sprang open again. She passed through, her eyes adjusting to the relative darkness of the library.

She looked around. Graham had already pushed his way to the front of the line at the check-out desk.

"Pipe down, lady," he was saying to an irate woman behind him. "Police business."

"Look, can I help you?" said a young man behind the counter. His eyebrows were knotted in anger. He was also, Della noticed, unhealthily thin.

She approached him before Graham could bite the guy's head off.

"I'm terribly sorry." She smiled sweetly. "It's a rather urgent matter. We were wondering if you could tell us where we might find a particular book. *Cat's Curiosity,* by Bertrand Powell."

The young man softened. He typed something into his computer. "Uh, yeah. Let me see… Our only copy was checked out a little while ago."

Graham thumped the counter hard. "Damn it!"

Della flinched. A little girl with pigtails stepped out from behind Graham and put her finger to her mouth, ready to *ssh* him.

Della caught her eye. She shook her head. The girl slunk away.

Graham leaned in and growled at the desk clerk. "Who took it?"

Della felt the urge to translate. "Is there any chance you could tell us the address of the person who borrowed the book?"

The guy opened his mouth to answer.

A loud, terrified scream pierced the silence.

Della whirled around.

A teenage girl tumbled backward from one of the aisles and crumpled to her knees. She brought her hands up to her face, sobbing into them.

Graham bolted over to the aisle. Della followed.

She reached the girl and put a protective arm around her. "Are you okay?"

Della looked down the stacks. Graham was at the end of the aisle, kneeling over something. She tried to get a better look. Her view was obstructed by a small crowd, gathering around the girl. Offering comfort.

Graham turned back and made eye contact with her. His skin was gray.

Please don't vomit again, Della thought, bracing herself.

He motioned for her to come over.

She left the girl in the care of an elderly man with a kind face. She headed down the stacks.

She saw the bottom half of a woman's legs, her shoes pointing upward. It made her think of the striped socks and ruby slippers of the Wicked Witch of the East, poking out from beneath Dorothy's house in *The Wizard of Oz.*

Graham moved out of the way.

She was in her sixties, Della guessed. Her hair was dyed a chestnut brown and looked faintly ridiculous next to her white, waxy skin. Dried tear tracks ran from the woman's half-closed eyes and disappeared into the cracks of her cheeks.

She had that look, Della realized. Like she was not a *she* at all. Just a discarded shell.

Della knelt down. She saw something else.

She clamped a hand to her mouth.

"Oh, no..."

Graham was intrigued. "What is it?"

Della pulled aside the collar of the woman's cardigan. She struggled to make sense of what she was seeing. She cupped her forehead in her hand. Moved her fingers down and rubbed her eyes.

"What is it?" Graham repeated.

She would have to call Donna. Tell her she wouldn't be able to make it. There was nothing she could do now.

The vacation was cancelled.

Graham was getting impatient now. "Hello?"

She didn't hear him. She was busy studying the marks on the woman's skin. Deep burns that circled her neck.

Burns that could only have been made by a noose.

CHAPTER 15

Della stared into her tea. She swished the liquid around, watching the scum rise and fall as it clung to the sides of the mug. It had something to do with the chalk hills the town was built around, someone had once explained to her. It made the water smoky, and the tea undrinkable.

She looked up as April entered the living room. The girl wore pink pajamas decorated with fairies, and her eyes were puffy with sleep. Della felt terrible for once again disturbing the poor girl, but April brightened when she saw her. Her smile promptly vanished, however, when she saw Graham sitting in the armchair alongside Della.

Della had asked him to stay in the car, but as she'd expected, he was having none of it. "Let me do the talking," she had ordered him as they stood on the doorstep. He had glared back, but she didn't care. God only knows what kind of mess they would be in if she let him handle things.

"This isn't what you think it is," he had responded, and his tone was strangely sorrowful. "It's something far, far worse."

Della wasn't sure, thinking back, if she had tutted or rolled her eyes at that moment. Probably both. If there was one thing she was beginning to learn about Graham, it was that he had a flair for the melodramatic.

Remembering his words now, though, she felt a chill drive its way through her. Shortly after leaving the library she had explained to him about the marks around Elizabeth Paul's neck, and had shared her theory that there was a serial killer on the loose in the sleepy town of Chalkstone. What, she wondered, could possibly be far, far worse than that?

Della placed her mug on a coaster and vacated the chair beside Graham. She crossed the room and sat next to April on the couch.

"If it's okay," she said softly, "I have a question I need to ask you. About last night."

She thought about taking April's hand in hers, but she didn't want to seem too familiar. Before she could decide, the girl grabbed Della's hand and squeezed it tight.

"Just you," April whispered, her eyes flitting over toward Graham but not looking at him.

Della smiled. She stroked the back of April's hand. "I want you to think real hard, okay? Was there anyone else with you in the house last night? Before you met with me and the other police lady?"

April frowned. "Lizzie."

"That's right. Anyone else?"

April shook her head.

"Anyone else at all? It's okay, you can tell me."

She paused for a moment. She shook her head.

"Are you sure?"

She nodded.

"You never saw anyone else, all evening?"

April shook her head rapidly. "Nobody."

Della looked into her eyes. "Okay." She took a sip of tea, and grimaced. She hid it with a smile. "Okay. Thank you. You've been very helpful."

April tightened her grip. "Nobody real."

Della's smile stiffened.

She heard the armchair creak as Graham leaned forward.

She motioned for him to keep back. "What do you mean, sweetie?"

"You said it yourself," the girl said. "What's in the book isn't real. It's just make believe."

"That's right. That's right, it is." She felt April's fingers trembling beneath hers. "Did you see something? In the book?"

April shuffled closer, her breath quickening. "She was in the drawing."

"Who was?"

"The lady. And then...she was real."

"Real?"

"Yeah. She was right there. At my bedroom window."

Graham gasped. "What did she look like?"

Della whirled round. "Graham..."

April thought for a moment. "Like she had just gotten out of bed."

"What color was her hair?" he asked.

"Graham!" Della barked. "Please."

"I don't know," April said. "I couldn't tell."

Della stroked the girl's hand. "That's okay, don't worry, it doesn't matter."

Graham continued. "Blonde? Brunette?"

"It was too dark."

"Was she a redhead?"

"I don't know."

"She was a redhead, wasn't she?"

"I don't know."

"Was it long hair?"

Della leapt to her feet. "Stop it, Graham!"

He moved toward April. "It's not a difficult question. Long or short?"

April flinched, shrinking back against the couch. Della darted in between the two of them. She pushed her hands against Graham's chest. "Back off, buddy. Back off. Right now!"

Graham batted her hands away, still talking to April. "Other lives are in danger here, do you understand?"

"You heard me," Della demanded.

April got to her feet, struggling to get away from him. "I don't know what I can tell you, just please..."

Della glared at Graham. She held him at arm's length. "We're leaving. You got that?"

"Just leave me alone," April screamed. "Both of you!"

She ran from the room. Della heard her crying as she thumped up the stairs.

Della turned to Graham, seething with anger. Her top lip curled into a scowl.

He stared back, wide-eyed. "What?"

***

They approached the car. Graham unlocked it and opened the driver's side door.

Della elbowed him out of the way. "Don't even think about it."

She slid in behind the wheel.

Graham turned without fuss and walked around to the other side of the vehicle. He climbed into the front passenger seat and closed the door.

They sat in silence as Della pulled the lever beneath the driver's seat, sliding it forward. She adjusted the rearview mirror.

Graham watched her. "You believe me now though, right? We have to get that book."

She untangled the pine tree air freshener from the rearview mirror, wound down the side window and threw it out.

"Hey!" Graham yelled. "I like that!"

She clipped in her seat belt and started the engine. Threw the car into gear.

She paused and turned to him.

He glanced back at her. "What?"

"Tell me."

"Tell you what?"

She locked eyes on him.

Graham was disconcerted. "What?"

She continued to stare.

He broke her gaze. "There's no time."

"Sure there is."

"Trust me. You don't want to hear it."

"Oh, but I do."

He tapped his watch. "We have to go. Now."

"Tell me on the way."

He looked back. She was still watching him. He flinched.

The engine purred as the car sat, idling.

Della drummed her fingers on the steering wheel.

He huffed. "Fine."

The tires squealed as Della peeled away from the curb. She joined the flow of traffic headed into town.

"So come on, then," Della said. "Who is she?"

CHAPTER 16

"Miriam's favorite place in the whole world was the garden I built for her in the spring of ninety-two. It had trellis walls and a beamed ceiling that shot out at an angle from the side of our house, with a felt roof that you rolled back in the summer. Before that we'd had nothing but a concrete yard and a dilapidated shed, no lawn to speak of. It was almost a deal-breaker for her when we bought the place, but I promised I'd sort something out.

"Well anyway, she loved it. I'd often find her out there when I got home from work, potting plants or rearranging the furniture. She was into feng shui before anybody really knew what it was. Sometimes she'd just be out there on the iron bench, reading a magazine or meditating.

"I came home one time, after a particularly shitty day if I recall, and she sat me down out there. She had tears in her eyes, and this look… I couldn't decipher it. My heart was beating fast, thinking about all the terrible things it could be. I asked her what was wrong, and she laughed. 'No, silly,' she said. 'They're happy tears.' And that's when she told me."

Graham sighed. Della glanced over.

"She was pregnant. It was a shock, no two ways about it. We hadn't been trying, nor was it anything we'd ever really discussed. But it seemed right. As if all this time something had been missing from our lives, and we'd never quite pinpointed what it was. I remember clear as anything Miriam sitting on my lap out there, giggling as I wiped away her tears. I remember because I didn't have her for much longer. Something snapped, something fundamental, and before long she was not the woman I'd married. Less than a week, I think it was, before the trouble started.

"It was only at night to begin with. I've never been a great sleeper, so I didn't miss a thing that first time. In retrospect, I probably wasn't as understanding as I could have been. She shot bolt upright, scaring the living hell out of me, and she was soaked with sweat, just like in the movies when somebody has a nightmare. She was shouting like a crazy person, and I tried to calm her, but when I grabbed her arm, she was, you know, convulsing."

"A seizure?"

"Right. Or at least, that's what it seemed like to me. I was all ready to call the doctor, let me tell you. But then she fixed me with a stare, and she spoke slowly and carefully, and she said, 'the baby's going to die.'

"I'll admit, in the moment it was pretty terrifying. But the next morning I came down and she was making toast. We sat there and ate our breakfast and she had a bee in her bonnet about the neighbor's cats, and how they had crapped in her plant pots again. Not a single mention of the night before. Well, I certainly wasn't going to bring it up. And that was that.

"A couple of months later her mother came to visit. Lydia was kind of a plump version of Miriam, but she was still a good-looking woman. I always figured if Miriam looked like her mother when she got to be her age, well, that wouldn't be such a bad thing. Anyway, Lydia was real excited. It was her first grandchild, after all. She brought a little present wrapped in pink paper. I don't know if she knew something we didn't or what, but anyhow, Miriam opened it and it was the book she had read over and over as a child. Her favorite book. *Cat's Curiosity*, by Bertrand Powell. It was old and battered, even then - there were scratches in the leather and the corners were scuffed - but she adored it.

"She flicked through the book and sniffed the pages, as if that god-awful musty stench was the smell of a rose garden or something, and then she started quoting passages from memory, and Lydia joined in. *Cat was a curious little girl, with a pinafore dress and a cutesy curl* - blah de blah de blah. They were giggling and hugging, and I didn't really get it. It was a mother-daughter thing, I suppose. Lydia explained that the book had been passed down the generations, that her mother had read it to her, and her mother before that, and now she was passing it down to our little one. Miriam was crying by this point. She thanked her and promised she would treasure it forever, and they hugged again.

"Over dinner, Lydia asked if we had any names yet. Well, I looked over at Miriam and she was just stiff as a board. She glanced back at me and I could see it in her eyes. That's when I knew - all this time, she had remembered. She muttered something about not thinking that far ahead, and then she turned the color of rotten pork and excused herself from the table.

"I gave it a little while and then I went up to see if she was alright. When I walked in the room she was rocking back and forth on the edge of the bed, saying 'she's in danger,' over and over again. I thought she was talking about her mother. 'No,' she said, 'our daughter. Our daughter is in danger. Our daughter is going to die.'

"I tell you, I'm not good with mad shit like that. 'This is crazy,' I said. 'It doesn't mean anything. You're not psychic, you can't predict the future. It's just your fears rising to the surface, your fears of being a mother. It's natural. Maybe it's a hormone thing.'

"'Yes,' she said. 'That's precisely what it is. It's a hormone thing.' And she told me a story. Throughout puberty, a bunch of weird things had happened. From about the age of eight - she went through puberty real early, apparently - to age thirteen, she had a spate of psychic premonitions. Most of it was everyday, inconsequential stuff, like guessing the toy in the cereal or knowing the answers in a school test.

"But one summer the family went to a theme park, and there was this safari car ride. Fake jungle, that sort of thing. They all wanted to go on it. All except Miriam, that is. She screamed the moment she saw it. It wasn't long before she was hysterical, and her dad grabbed her and tried to keep her under control, and her mom was embarrassed and told her she was making a scene. But she wouldn't stop screaming. She said that Yasmin, her sister, was going to get hurt, that they mustn't go on the ride. Her dad told her not to be so bloody ridiculous, but Miriam refused to have any part of it, so he stayed with her while Lydia and Yasmin waited in line. But the guy controlling the ride, he was just a teenager himself, and he wasn't paying attention. So when Yasmin climbed aboard, the car moved off before she was properly inside, and she got her leg trapped between the car and the control booth.

"Now this guy, he was totally oblivious, still pulling the lever, trying to get the car to move, and Yasmin was screaming, and her parents were hollering at the guy to stop the ride, and all the time Miriam was on the floor yelling *why didn't you listen? Why didn't you listen?* And that's when they all heard this loud, sickening snap, and poor Yasmin's leg folded behind her. She was in hospital for a month, and in plaster for another three. She never walked properly again.

"Well, after that, of course, you can imagine. I was always going to be fighting an uphill battle. I told Miriam that it had all been just a series of coincidences, that psychic premonitions were a load of baloney, that she had nothing to worry about. But she reckoned she had further proof, because by her early teens, when her hormones had settled back down, the psychic feelings just went away. And now they had returned.

"She tried to convince me that everything she was feeling was as strong as the premonitions she had experienced back then. That the baby was in grave danger. But the whole time, I was thinking that maybe the pregnancy had awoken something that had been lying dormant in her brain. Not some psychic power, but something psychotic.

"And that's how it continued for a while. The more she worried for the baby, the more freaked out she became, the more I feared for her sanity. It got to the point where she was so paranoid, she wanted the baby checked out at the hospital. And I figured that might not be such a bad idea. If it gave her peace of mind, then great. And maybe I could, you know, speak to the doctor about her while we were there.

"Halfway to the hospital I pulled up at a set of traffic lights. We'd been sitting there a couple of minutes when I heard her say, 'Oh, my God.'

"I asked her what was wrong and she said, 'Look.' She pointed over to the left. I looked around and I couldn't see anything. 'There,' she said. 'The car, it's on fire.' I craned my neck and I still couldn't see anything, and then she turned her head slowly, from left to right, as if she was watching this car pass by in front of us. But I saw nothing.

"Just as I was thinking we needed to get to the hospital fast so we could get her some medication, she screamed. 'No, no, watch out, it's going to hit…' And she dived for cover. Well, I was just watching all this, bewildered, one eye on the traffic lights, waiting for them to change. And she climbed out of my lap, looking around as if waking from a dream, and said, 'It's green.'

"I was thinking this was still part of her performance, until of course I heard a car honking its horn behind me, and I looked and the light had gone green. So I moved on, but now I was on edge, because I was thinking, what if she does have psychic premonitions? I was looking around for burning cars, thinking we were going to have a bloody accident.

"Anyway, we made it to the hospital in one piece, and after a while we were shown into a cubicle, and a midwife felt her bump, she felt around quite hard, and she checked the baby's position. She strapped on a fetal heart monitor so that she could detect the baby's heartbeat. We could see it on the little screen, and Miriam panicked. The midwife assured her that everything was normal, but Miriam still thought the baby's heartbeat was too fast. Although she kept saying *her*. 'Her heartbeat.' I told her it was too early for anyone to know the sex of the baby, but she said she knew. And she said it with such conviction that I believed her.

"The midwife told us that she was going to monitor the baby for a while to make sure everything was okay, and she left us. But as soon as she closed the curtain, Miriam went absolutely nuts. She said that the midwife didn't know what she was talking about, that our daughter was in danger. Tears were streaming down her face. I tried calming her but I was embarrassed as well, 'cause I knew everyone could hear. I asked her to keep it down, but of course that only made her louder.

"And then, right in the middle of it all, an alarm went off. And the graph that had been spooling out of the machine suddenly flatlined. Well, I tell you, that shut her up. She looked over at me, and I could see the terror in her eyes, and I just… I couldn't help but wonder if maybe she did know something. But just as I was about to go and get help, the curtain pulled back, and it was the midwife, and she adjusted the position of the monitor, and there was the heartbeat again. She said the baby had moved inside her, that was all, and the monitor wasn't picking it up.

"I was so relieved. I think I was shaking at this point. 'See,' I said, like I had never doubted it for a second. 'Nothing's wrong. The baby's going to be fine.'

"Miriam squeezed my hand and smiled at me, but I could see she wasn't right. She motioned for me to move closer, so I did, and she whispered in my ear. And what she said…"

Graham paused. Della took her eyes away from the road for a second.

His breath shook as he sighed. "Well, it still turns my guts to ice. 'It's not just the baby,' she said. 'I'm going to die, too.'"

CHAPTER 17

"I refused to speak to her for much of the next hour. It was still pretty frosty between us on the drive home. Needless to say, I wasn't the most aware I've ever been behind the wheel. We stopped at an intersection, and I sat there, staring into space, chewing on peppermint gum and praying to God that she wasn't psychic, because if she was, then I knew I'd lost them both.

"And that's when it happened. For real this time.

"'Oh, my God,' she yelled, and I snapped out of my daydream, if that's what you call it - I don't know that there's a word for a waking nightmare. Anyway, I looked up, and there it was, slowly rolling along, crossing our path. A midnight blue VW Golf, and it was on fire. It just trundled past like it was the most ordinary thing in the world, and we watched it go. It skipped the red light and continued on across the junction. It was quite hypnotic.

"There was an almighty roar, and this other car, I think it was a BMW, approached real fast and only saw the Golf when it was too late. It smashed into the side of it, ricocheting off at such force that it shot onto the median strip and then up into the air.

"That's when Miriam screamed. 'No, no, watch out, it's going to hit...' And I could only watch as the BMW clipped a traffic light and flipped, sailing through the air, really quite graceful when I picture it, like a gymnast vacating the parallel bars. And it looked for all the world like it was going to come down on top of us. I tell you now, I thought I was a goner. So of course, we both dived for cover, like that would do us any good, and then there was a terrible bang, and I thought it had hit us. In fact, it landed back in the road alongside us, and when I looked up there was this awful squeal and all I saw was a great big BMW skidding along on its roof past the passenger window.

"Naturally, doing what I do, I stayed a while, helped out. The guy in the Beemer was not in a good way, unsurprisingly. I waited for my colleagues to arrive, and I told them all about what had happened. And the whole time I felt pretty wobbly inside, because now I knew the truth. She'd been right all along. She *was* fucking psychic.

"Obviously, we had to do something about it. But I just didn't know what. So I turned the car around and we went straight back to the hospital. And all the way there Miriam was freaking out, asking if I needed any more proof, begging me to understand that the baby was in danger, that the baby was going to die. I mean, Christ, I did my best, I tried to reassure her that it was nothing, that the accident was just a coincidence, that it wasn't proof of anything. But I didn't really believe that, and she knew it.

"Back at the hospital we told Miriam's doctor what had happened, and he looked at us like we were a pair of idiots. But I guess he wanted us out of his hair, because he recommended this other guy. Doctor Henning. He was a parapsychologist who studied extrasensory perception. I had no idea what any of that meant, but it sounded impressive, so we went over to see him. He was a squat little man with a combover, one of those guys with no discernible chin. His head just sort of continued down into his neck. And I tell you what, for a doctor he looked pretty sickly. His skin was as gray as the tank top he wore beneath his white coat.

"I told him we thought Miriam was psychic, and he was pretty full of himself, this guy. He started on about how, in his opinion, what science knew about the nature of the universe was incomplete, and how the limitations of human potential had been underestimated, and blah de blah de blah. And then he winked. 'But keep it under your hat,' he said. 'Don't want people thinking I'm a loon.'

"So now I was wondering what we'd got ourselves into, here. I was just about ready to leave. But he sat us down, and we ended up telling him the whole story. All of Miriam's visions. The stuff about the baby and her sister and the car crash. By this point, Henning was wriggling in his chair and looking uncomfortable. 'You know,' he said, 'really, I'm a psychologist. That's what they pay me for. I only lecture on parapsychology.'

"I was fuming. I got to my feet and I asked him straight out if we were wasting our time. He looked at me for a bit, rubbed his chin - it was in there somewhere, I guess - and said, 'wait here.'

"He brought out some cards. Plain on one side, with a picture on the other: a star, a circle, a square, a cross, wavy lines. I'm sure you've seen them."

"ESP cards."

"Right. That makes sense. Anyway, so he placed a chair over on one side of the room and sat at his desk on the other. He told Miriam to go sit in the chair, and he motioned for me to come and stand over him. He held up a card, a five-pointed star, so that we could see it but Miriam couldn't. And then he asked her to tell him what was on the card.

"Well, she just shrugged. 'It doesn't work like this,' she said. 'The flashes are random. I can't just do it to order.'

"'Listen to me, Miriam,' Henning said. 'Concentrate your mind. You can do this.'

"She flailed about for a bit, and I felt for her, and then she said, 'I don't know, triangle.'

"Henning laughed. 'But there isn't even a triangle card,' he said. That was pretty embarrassing. Miriam got up and started pacing the room and said she wanted to leave. I asked her if she could just give it another try, and if it wasn't working, then we'd go. So she sat back down, and Henning held up the card, and she stared at the back of it, and then her face...

"It changed, as if something had come over her, and she said, certain as anything, 'wavy lines.'

"I looked down at the card, 'cause, you know, she had me convinced, even though I knew it was a star.

"Henning gave me a little look, and he said, 'good,' and he flipped the card over and showed her. She didn't seem at all bothered that she got it wrong.

"He held up the next card. It was a square. 'Take your time,' he said.

"But she came back immediately with, 'circle.'

"Henning nodded. 'Good.' He showed her the card.

"I was pretty thrilled by this. Anything that proved she wasn't psychic had to be a good thing. But Henning continued the test anyway. He picked up the next one. Wavy lines this time.

"She was in the zone now, and she said, 'cross.'

"'Good,' he said, and flipped it over. Onto the next one. A circle.

"'Square,' she said.

"By this time I was starting to get embarrassed for her. I mean, even I could have guessed one right by now. So I whispered to Henning that we should end it. He held up his hand to silence me. Before he had even picked up the next card, she was already predicting it.

"'Wavy lines.' Henning picked up the card, and it was a cross. But Miriam didn't care. She was just gone. As if in a trance. Chanting shapes in a steady rhythm. 'Star... Circle... Cross... Star...'

"Henning was trying to keep up, rifling through the cards. 'It's okay,' I called to her. 'Miriam, it's okay. Don't worry, sweetheart. The test is over.'

"But she didn't hear me. 'Circle... Square... Cross... Circle...'

"Henning tapped me on the arm. He was watching Miriam, mesmerized. 'Watch this,' he said.

"Before he had even touched the next card, he said, 'square.' He picked it up, and it was a square. 'Wavy lines.' And sure enough, the next card was wavy lines. He did it again. 'Star.' And again. 'Circle.'

"I was amazed. Turns out Henning was bloody psychic. I asked him how the hell he was doing that. He twisted his chair around, and he looked up at me, and I could see his hand was shaking. I got real nervous and suddenly I wasn't even sure that I wanted an answer.

"'I know what's on each card,' he said, 'because your wife has already told me.'

"I looked over to her, and she was still in the zone, chanting cards. I asked him what he meant.

"'She has been predicting two cards into the future this whole time,' he said. 'She has the most incredible gift I have ever seen.'"

CHAPTER 18

Della missed her turning and cursed herself. She'd been so enraptured by Graham's story that she had lost her concentration for a few moments. Never mind. There was another turning up ahead, but it would add an extra few minutes to their journey. Maybe Graham wouldn't even notice.

He didn't seem to.

"I refused to let Miriam out of my sight for the rest of the pregnancy. Although I admit I made an exception when she went into labor. I just couldn't bring myself to go into the delivery room that night. I let the doctors handle her. And she was quite the handful, I later learned. Turns out they'd had to sedate her. But it seemed to me that if ever there was going to be a time when I would lose them both, it would have been then. I mean, it was the early nineteen-nineties, not the Middle Ages, and women didn't routinely die in childbirth, but still...

"I must have sat in that waiting room reading the same page of a magazine over and over for about four hours. But unlike all the many others who had waited in that same chair, I wasn't filled with the giddy excitement of an expectant father. More the numb anguish of a grieving husband. I was convinced that I had seen her alive for the last time, and - this is a pretty awful thing to admit - I felt overcome with an anger and bitterness towards the baby, who I felt for certain was about to kill my beautiful wife. I didn't care, right then, if the kid lived or died. I'd already prepared myself for the worst. But I wanted my Miriam back.

"Of course, everything changed shortly afterwards, when I met the new arrival. She was a stunningly gorgeous little thing with big blue eyes, just like her mother. If I'm honest, at the time I didn't even know newborn babies opened their eyes so soon, I thought it was a gradual thing. But here she was, little Miss Nosey, looking around, at me, at her surroundings, taking it all in. It was clear to me immediately that she was going to have an inquisitive nature. She was a natural for the force. I could already picture that inevitable day when I'd be there on the sidelines, the proud father, watching her during her passing out parade.

"I named her there in the room, while Miriam was still out of it. *My Cherie Amour.* Given that I never thought the day would come when I'd be holding her in my arms, I almost felt I had a duty to call her something like Hope or Faith or Miracle. But when I looked at her, there was one song that kept playing in my head like a stuck record. So Cherie it was.

"Given her mental state, Miriam was kept in under observation for a week while I took the baby home. 'This kind of episode,' the doctor said to me as I packed Cherie's bag, 'is more common than you realize. Just a few hormones whizzing around. Nothing to be alarmed about. She'll be right as rain in no time at all.' I just nodded along and made agreeable noises at the appropriate times. What could I say?

"It was fun, though, those first few days with just Cherie and I. In truth, I'd been so worried about the baby that I hadn't prepared much for the realities of fatherhood. I hadn't wanted to jinx it. But I stumbled through, like we all have to, and I changed nappies - sorry, diapers - and prepared bottles and made the necessary adjustments to my sleeping routine. But as joyful and challenging as it was, I couldn't wait for us to be a family again.

"When I collected Miriam from the hospital, I couldn't believe it. It was as if I had ordered a new wife. She was so excited to see the baby, of course, and there was no hint of - well, you know... the madness. I was suspicious, no doubt about it. I kept looking for signs that she was faking it. But they simply were not there. She had that old twinkle in her eyes again, something I thought had been lost forever, and I felt like the luckiest bastard alive. That young doctor was right. It was as if the pregnancy had caused all of her issues, and now that it was over a switch had been flicked, and her mind was free again.

"If only I could have forgotten so easily. The horror of what could have been woke me up more times in the night than the baby did. The paranoia was immense. I found myself sneaking into Cherie's room at all hours just to check on her, to make sure she was still breathing. But I didn't say anything to Miriam. She seemed to be taking motherhood in her stride, and I didn't want to rock the boat.

"About a week or so later I came home from work, parked in the garage as always, and when I got out of the car something caught my eye. There was a little note on the chest freezer we kept out there. Just a piece of lined paper that had been ripped from a jotter and taped to the lid. There were three words etched onto it in shaky handwriting:

don't look inside

"I chuckled. That was typical of Miriam. The old Miriam, that is, and it sent a warm feeling through me, knowing that she was back. She was always leaving notes about the place, like *don't forget your lunch* or *wake me in an hour* or simply *love you, big guy.*

"I looked down at her latest note. My birthday was coming up in a week's time and I figured she'd had to hide my present. Although I couldn't think what she could have bought me that required freezer storage. And I couldn't put my finger on it, but there was something not quite right about that note, something about the way it was written. It made me uneasy.

"I dropped my stuff and went into the house. It was silent. When you have a newborn baby, that's not such an unusual thing. I guessed they were both asleep upstairs. Then I saw something while I was out there in the hall, through the gap in the door. Movement.

"I stepped through into the dining room and Miriam was there in the corner. Slumped down against the wall, rocking back and forth. She was breathing noisily, too. Sucking in on the rock back and exhaling sharply as she came forward.

"I felt so sick the words almost didn't come out. 'Where's the baby?'

"She kept rocking, as if I wasn't there. I thought perhaps she couldn't see me, because her hair was in her eyes. I moved closer. That's when I realized that she wasn't breathing noisily, she was actually saying something as she swayed. One word, over and over. 'Evil, evil, evil, evil, evil, evil, evil, evil…'

"By this time I was frantic. 'Where's the baby?' I shouted. She stopped rocking with a jerk and fell silent, as if the word she had been repeating had lodged itself in her throat. She slowly lifted her eyes to mine.

"The look she gave me will haunt me for the rest of my days. She jutted her bottom lip out in an expression of childlike remorse. As if she had been caught with her hand in the cookie jar. 'It was evil,' she said, a runner of dribble hanging from her chin. I asked her what she was talking about, and she bit her lip. 'I was fine,' she said. 'Until I got pregnant. Everything was fine. We were fine. It was only when that *thing* started growing inside me...'

"My stomach twisted up. I almost buckled. I think I knew everything, then, but I didn't want to believe it. I turned and got out of there. She called after me, but her voice was raspy and I couldn't make out the words.

"I fell over at one point - my head was woozy - but I got straight back up again, my heart thumping hard in my chest, and went out the back.

don't look inside

"I couldn't do it. I wanted to be anywhere else. But my hands gripped the lid of the freezer anyway, as if moving of their own accord. I stared down at that handwritten note. There were several puncture holes in the paper where the nib of the pen had pressed down too hard.

don't

"My fingers wrapped tight around the handle and pulled up against the resistance of the lid.

look

"A fine mist of vapor escaped the cabinet as I opened the lid to the full extent that its hinges would allow. I braced myself and looked down.

"There is a protective mechanism inside all of us that simply won't allow us to process certain images in the moment of their discovery. The brain is a complex organ with a multitude of tasks to complete at any given second, and sometimes it needs to throw up that firewall. Certain stimuli are like viruses that take root in the mind and gobble up great gobs of sanity as they spread. That's what I believe, anyway, and that is my explanation for why I found myself, some immeasurable period of time later, propped up against the back wall of the garage, a toolbox digging in my back and the rung of a stepladder acting as a ridged metal pillow for my head.

"I groaned, righted myself, and rubbed my aching neck. The lid of the chest freezer was wide open only a couple of yards away, and that's when my mind screamed, and my vision exploded into blobs of light, and the full force of what had happened

(chunks of meat)

came down on me in one swift and brutal motion. I heard a terrible yelping that became all the more frightening when I realized that it was escaping my own mouth. I stumbled to my feet, falling against the hood of the car, edging around it so that I wouldn't have to look over to my right.

"But I could still see the freezer at the edge of my vision. Its unspeakable contents flashed before me like a hideous strobe.

"I found Miriam outside, in her garden, as I so often had done on my return from work. Only this time, she was hanging from the beamed roof, her eyes bulging but lifeless, her body tiny and frail, suspended there. The noose had slipped, revealing a raw track that circled her neck.

"My knees came unhinged and I crumpled to the floor. Her toes brushed past my shoulder, causing me to scream, and as I hunched down farther onto those cold stone slabs I began to cry. Big, gasping sobs that seemed like they would never stop. That was, until my elbow touched something. When I was done and ready to open my eyes again, I looked over.

"The book. There it was, and had been, all the time, directly beneath her body. *Cat's Curiosity*, by Bertrand Powell. Lydia's gift to our daughter.

"I picked it up and studied the cover. The girl with the branches protruding from her ears. Branches weighed heavy with plump apples. I ran the pads of my fingers over the grooves in the embossed illustration. As my hand moved across the leather, something else appeared. Deep scratches that formed a word.

DON'T

"I jolted upright. Miriam kicked me in the head. The rope creaked. A wood pigeon cooed somewhere.

"I had already anticipated what was coming - that note on the freezer lid sprang to mind as soon as I saw that first word - and sure enough, the rest of the warning appeared before my eyes.

LOOK
INSIDE

"I threw the book down. You might not be entirely surprised to hear that I vomited. And yet, even as I retched and spat my hot bile into one of Miriam's potted plants, my hands scrabbled for the book. I groped the spine and pulled it toward me. My fingers pawed at the edge of the cover. What *was* inside? I had to know."

CHAPTER 19

Della tore her concentration away from the road and glanced over at Graham. At first she thought he was taking a dramatic pause before the big reveal. But it turned out he had just stopped talking.

He was staring out the side window, his forehead resting on the glass, his breath fogging the view. A broken man.

Della opened her mouth to speak, and then hesitated. She didn't want to seem insensitive - his head was no doubt swirling with long-repressed emotions, and her heart ached for him - but still, he couldn't leave her in suspense like that. It wasn't fair.

"Well?"

He turned and looked at her. His expression suggested, for a few moments, that he had no idea who she was. "Well what?"

"What was inside?"

He blinked hard. He was back. "Right. Yeah."

Della returned her attention to the road. They were only a few streets from their destination now, and she hadn't even realized. Graham's tale had certainly made for an interesting journey.

Finally, he spoke. "I never opened the book. The allure was strong, but somehow, this time, I resisted. I'd learned my lesson. When I'd seen those same three words on the note on the freezer, I had given in to temptation, and it had destroyed me. I wasn't going to make that same mistake again. There was a force at work as I looked at the message on the cover, something powerful, but I wasn't going to let it take me. I threw the book down, and the words - well, they were gone. Of course, thinking about it later, it made perfect sense that I had imagined the warning on the cover."

"Because of the note?"

"Right. That handwritten note, those three words - they were seared into my brain. Etched onto my retinas. I had projected them onto the book, that was all. I knew the drill; I'd been through it enough times with others. I'd suffered an intense trauma, I was wracked with grief, I wasn't right in the head. A trick of the mind, that's all it had been. I convinced myself of that fact for more than twenty years. Stood by it when the voice in my head tried to persuade me otherwise. Until today. When that little girl described the book… That's when I knew."

Della's mind sprang back to the interview room. Graham's hands gripped vice-tight to the edge of the table. His rigidity as she touched his shoulder. She shivered as she realized he had been frozen with fear.

Looking back, knowing what she knew now, the projectile vomiting had seemed like a relatively restrained response. "What happened to the book?"

Graham sighed. His breath was shaking. "Like all of Cherie's stuff, I couldn't stand to keep it in the house. I guess others in my situation would have wanted to be surrounded by memories and mementoes, but not me. I had a big yard sale. Didn't care what price anything went for. I think I damn well near gave it all away. Sick bastards, really, if you think about it. They all knew what had happened, my ghoulish neighbors, and there they all were, clambering for keepsakes."

"Did you sell all of Miriam's stuff, too?"

His lip curled into a sneer. "No. I made a big pile of her things out back, lit a match and watched it burn. I wanted no trace to remain of that child killing bitch. Clearly, I should have burned the book as well. I just thought of it as Cherie's, you know?"

Della nodded. She let the silence hang for a moment.

She had something difficult to ask him. She felt incredibly awkward even broaching the subject, and she didn't want Graham to bite her head off, but it had to be done.

"You really think it's Miriam? You think... You think she's somehow inside that book?"

"I know, I know. And if we were anywhere else in the world, then I'd be inclined to share your skepticism. But I tell you, it's this town. Chalkstone. There's something seriously wrong with this place. There always has been." He paused for a moment. "Have you ever been down to the cell block after dark?"

Della opened her mouth to speak. She wanted to tell him about her recent experience, but nothing came out.

Graham accepted her silence as a response. "If you had, then you'd know. You'd understand that I'm not just a stupid old fool. Your mind would be more open to..." He stopped.

Della clung to his every word. *Open to...*

He batted away the thought with his hand. "Well, anyway, that right there is why I refuse to work the night shift."

Screeee—screeee—screeee—screeee—

She was back there. That awful heaviness in the air. She blinked the memory away.

But the sound remained, louder now.

Screeee—screeee—screeee—screeee—

It wasn't the alarm, it was her phone, ringing.

She jumped. Scrambled to answer it. She was grateful for the distraction. "Hello?"

"Della?" It was Harlan. "Is this a good time? I was hoping to catch you before the flight."

She deflated inside. *Thanks for the reminder, buddy.* "No, it's fine. What's up?"

"Well, I hope you're ready for something weird."

Oh, good. "Go on."

"Okay, so… The babysitter. Elizabeth Paul. There are no signs of intracranial bleedings, no cerebral contusions."

"Meaning?"

"Meaning it wasn't the fall that killed her."

Della took this in. She was almost afraid to ask the next question. "So, what was the cause of death?"

"Pressure on the jugular vein backed up the blood in her brain, resulting in unconsciousness and depressed respiration. That same pressure on the larynx cut off air flow to the lungs, producing asphyxia."

"She was hanged?"

"Right. I mean, we assumed the rope burns were from an earlier incident, because they looked at least a day old. Turns out we were wrong. I don't know, maybe she was hanged first, then thrown down the stairs?"

"That makes no sense."

"Oh yeah? Well I haven't even got to the weird part."

"What?"

"Okay. So, the librarian. She had those same aged marks, right? Consistent with suicidal hanging. And you know what? Cause of death was identical."

"Wait, Harlan… I was there. There was no noose. She wasn't strung up."

"I know, and the physical evidence contradicts it, too. Rope burns like those on both victims only occur if the body has been left hanging for some considerable time. Which was not the case, at either crime scene. And yet - the cause of death suggests otherwise. It's illogical. It's as if, I don't know… "

Della stiffened. "A ghost did it."

The phone fell from her hand. It clattered into the footwell.

She could still hear Harlan on the other end. "Right, right, of course. Because that makes perfect sense. Hello? Hello? Della? Are you there?"

She turned to Graham. He was staring back, a fire of blazing intensity in his eyes. Clearly, he had pieced together enough of the conversation.

"What happened with Miriam's body?" she asked. "Did you cut her down?"

He snorted. "Did I hell. I let the bitch hang. Besides, I'm a cop, I'm not stupid. I knew I'd be the prime suspect if anything looked out of sorts. So I left her. Waited for my colleagues to arrive."

"How long after she hanged herself did you make the call?"

"I don't know. Like, the next day? You've got to understand, I blacked out, lost all track of time. Then after I saw her… I was in no state to be making phone calls for a while there."

Della nodded, but inside she was falling apart. *Jesus Christ.*

A thought ran repeatedly through her mind. A thought so ridiculous she instinctively fought against it.

The book really was haunted.

She steered the vehicle into a small parking lot and maneuvered into a space adjacent to a block of identical garage doors, all daubed with graffiti. Beyond the garages a concrete apartment building stretched high, out of her sight. She killed the engine.

"Come on," she said. "We're gonna go get that book back before someone else dies."

CHAPTER 20

Navigating the soulless concrete jungle of the apartment block reminded Della a lot of Wixoe Downs. This housing project was nothing like as vast as that South Boston monstrosity, but she couldn't help feeling, as she passed row after row of identical, paint-peeled doors, stopping occasionally to dip her head beneath taut washing lines crammed with permanently stained baby clothes, that it had that same stench of desperate living about it.

She felt safer here, for sure - on the day that she had climbed the stairwells of building seventeen of Wixoe Downs, her hand had been poised over her weapon the whole time - but being here brought back that same twisted feeling in her belly that she had endured as a detective two years earlier.

Graham stopped at a door a few apartments down, motioning for her to come. He had marched ahead impatiently, as was his way, and Della had let him. No sense in letting the sniffer dog strain on the leash if he's going to lead you to the payload. She caught up.

He rapped his fist on the door. A few seconds later he knocked again, harder this time.

A chain rattled on the other side of the door. A raspy female voice called out. "Alright, alright, hold your fuckin' horses."

A bolt snapped back and the whole door shuddered. It stuck in the frame for a moment and then swung open. A woman in her mid-fifties stood there. She wore faded jeans and cheap slippers. Her hair was wet. A pink vest clung to her sagging breasts.

Her face, gnarled with fury when the door had sprung open, uncoiled itself as she gazed upon the two officers. "Well shit in my hat, that was quick. I only called you guys two minutes ago."

Della's eyes narrowed. "You did?"

"Yeah. You're here about my daughter's kidnapping, right?"

Della looked at Graham. Graham looked right back. He shrugged.

"Yes, Madam," Della said. "Yes we are."

The woman stepped aside and waved them in. Della went first. A short and narrow hallway with a door either side led to a modest living room. Della entered and looked around. The decor was very 1970s. A musty smell hung in the air. She had heard that when this tower block was first built it had won an award for the most homes contained within the smallest area. Now she was inside, she could see why.

Graham entered and scanned the room. He marched over to a wall unit clogged with ornaments and trinkets.

The woman picked up a framed photograph from a side table and handed it to Della. "That's Rhiannon," she said, pointing to a girl in her twenties dressed like a children's beauty pageant winner. "And that fuckwit next to her is her supposed boyfriend, Vince. Mind my language. I'm Gwen, by the way."

"It's nice to meet you, Gwen."

"Would you care for a cup of tea? I just boiled the kettle."

Della winced, remembering her last brew. She still had a coating of chalk on her tongue. "I'm fine, thank you."

She examined the photo. Vince had a severe, close-cropped haircut and pockmarked skin. His sculpted arms displayed military tattoos. "You say your daughter was kidnapped?"

"Yeah, by crater face here."

Gwen looked up, distracted by Graham. He opened a cupboard and shut it again. Peered inside a drawer.

Gwen turned to Della. "What is he doing?"

Della handed back the photograph. "So let me just clarify. You think your daughter's been kidnapped by her boyfriend?"

"I know what it sounds like," Gwen snapped. "But he's not right in the head, see. He's a real whack job. I think the army twisted his noggin. Works in demolition now, though. Which is about right, 'cause he's destroyed my family. She's all I've got."

Graham crossed the room and opened a door.

Gwen gasped. "Don't go in there!"

He charged inside before she had finished speaking. She hurried after him. Della followed. She found Graham rifling through a closet in what looked like a young girl's bedroom. China dolls in pink dresses stared blankly from a wall of shelves.

"Don't you dare make a mess," Gwen demanded. "This is my baby's room. She's very particular."

Graham moved on to the nightstand and checked the drawer. "Where are your books?"

Gwen gawped at him. "You what?"

"Books. You borrowed some books. Where are they?"

Her eyebrows bunched together. "What are you? The library police?"

"I'm sorry, Gwen," Della said. "But it's important."

Gwen sighed. "Well, I don't do much in the way of reading. Rhiannon's the one with the library card. I think she took a whole bunch of books with her for the trip. That girl, bless her, she loves her fairy tales."

Graham froze mid-search.

He turned to her. "You're right," he said. He came over, smiling now. "You're absolutely right. Finding your daughter is our number one priority. Do you happen to know where they went?"

Gwen brightened considerably. She handed him the picture. "The Chalkstone Regatta," she said. "But that basket case will be up to no good, mark my words. That's why I called you lot. Don't want my girl embroiled in it."

Graham returned the picture to Gwen without looking at it. "I see. Tell me, what kind of vehicle does this charmer drive?"

Gwen's eyes widened. Her jaw dropped open, but no words came out. She drummed her fingers on her forehead. "Hang on. Wait… A blue one?"

Graham waited in silence, but nothing more was forthcoming. "You happen to know a make or model?"

"I know sweet Fanny Adams about cars, Mister," she said. "But I can get you the license plate details, if that helps?"

Graham shot Della a look. She could tell that he was desperate to roll his eyes.

"Yes, Gwen," he said. "Yes, that might be of some help."

Gwen scuttled out of the bedroom. Graham raised his eyebrows. "Colorful character."

Della tried to smile, but her face contorted into a grimace. She didn't have a good feeling about this, and she wasn't exactly sure why.

Sure. Kid yourself. You know why.

She tried to ignore that voice. She didn't need it right now.

Rhiannon's dead already. Burn marks around her neck. You know it, he knows it. And you'll be back here soon enough to break the news to her mother.

Gwen returned, slipping a piece of paper into Graham's large hand. She spun around and, to Della's surprise, grabbed her by the wrists.

"You promise me," Gwen said, staring deep into Della's eyes, her harsh tones softened now, "you'll get my Rhiannon back safe?"

Della looked down, awkward. She had been in this job long enough to know never to make promises.

She lifted her gaze to the worried mother before her.

"Try not to worry, Gwen," she said. "We'll do our best." She tried to resist anything further, but it came out anyway. "I'm sure your daughter will be just fine."

CHAPTER 21

The burnt-orange plumage of two extravagant headpieces crested the brow of the hill, accompanied by the rhythmic clip of hooves. There followed the nodding heads of a pair of magnificent beasts, from whose bridles the bright feathers sprung, and moments thereafter the glistening, golden carriage that was their cargo.

Inside, Princess Rhiannon beamed as she surveyed the countryside rolling before her. With delicate fingers wrapped in the silk of her elbow-length gloves, she removed from her purse an ornately framed hand mirror. Gazing upon the tumble of her hair in its crystal clear reflection, she corrected the angle of her jewel-encrusted tiara.

Satisfied, her eyes dropped to the final page of the weathered tome in her lap, and she devoured the words contained within:

Cat was a curious little girl
With a pinafore dress and a cutesy curl.
She got awfully dirty when out to play
And soaked in the tub at the end of each day.

"Don't bathe too long," mother warned her
"Or you'll be flushed out with the dirty water."
Cat was curious; how oddly pleasing!
She bathed until the water was freezing.

Out popped the plug with a gurgling sound
Cat swished and swirled and spun around.
Then with a burp she was sucked down the drain
And nobody ever saw Cat again.

"Splendid," the princess exclaimed. She closed her book, studying the embossed picture on its cover. The young girl in the illustration seemed to smile back at her. Rhiannon sighed sweetly, pressing the pages to her breast. She had discovered a new favorite read.

She gazed out of the carriage window, past the lush green meadow, where her eyes met a most pleasing sight.

"Oh my," she cried. "On the horizon. Isn't it magical?"

Her prince glanced over, his azure eyes sparkling, the symmetry of his facial features aligned perfectly with the cut of his chiseled cheekbones, and together the young couple feasted on the exquisite view. There stood a majestic castle, its outline seemingly ripped from the pages of a fairytale, its gleaming turrets piercing the caramel sky.

"Remarkable," he replied.

"And do you think that together we might, one day, make such a place our home?"

He took her dainty hand in his and kissed it softly.

"Your wish," he breathed, "is my command."

Rhiannon let slip a coy giggle, her eyes filling with joyful tears, her heart singing with romance.

She settled back for the ride, a contended smile dancing on the bow of her lips. She glanced down at the storybook, its weight now resting in the folds of her skirts.

There before her, etched deep into the leather, were three words.

Rhiannon gasped. She placed a trembling hand across her heaving décolletage and an exclamation of royal bewilderment burst forth from her exquisite mouth.

"What the fuck?"

***

The sharp angles of a 1981 Austin Princess chugged over the hill, the vehicle's slanting panels affording it a wedge-like appearance, its rust patches indistinguishable from the dirty orange of its battered bodywork. What it lacked in horsepower it made up for in sheer spectacle - it was, astounded residents of Chalkstone had often been heard to exclaim, one of the ugliest heaps of junk ever to disgrace the town's roads.

Inside the vehicle Rhiannon sneezed, wiped her nose on the back of her sleeve, and, with tobacco-stained fingers, adjusted the angle of the car's cracked side-view mirror. She gazed upon the knots of her ratty hair in its cobweb-strewn reflection, adjusting her faded pink headband.

Satisfied, her eyes dropped to the final page of the book in her lap: *Cat's Curiosity*, by Bertrand Powell. When she had finished reading she slammed the book shut and hugged it tight to her chest. She gazed out of the car's grubby side window, past featureless marshland, and saw something that pleased her.

"Oh my," she cried. "On the horizon. Isn't it magical?"

Her boyfriend Vince glanced over, his narrow gray eyes lifeless, the skin on his cheeks as bumpy as the land he surveyed was flat. He squinted, scanning the view for anything remarkable. He saw only the harsh silhouette of the Chalkstone water tower, a concrete monstrosity that was the closest thing this crappy town had to a landmark.

"Remarkable," he replied, returning his eyes to the road ahead.

"And do you think that together we might, one day, make such a place our home?"

He looked at her with alarm for a moment, then realized she was just being Rhiannon. "Your wish," he sighed, "is my command."

He loved the girl, and had always appreciated that she saw beauty in the mundane, even in this hellhole of a town, but she lived her life with her head permanently stuck in the clouds. She had no clue what the world was really like. In many ways he envied her that level of ignorance. Since returning from his tour of duty he had witnessed only the very worst that the world had to offer, and he had decided that enough was enough. It was time to take a stand.

He gazed back at his girlfriend and clocked the expression of horror etched onto her face. His heart leapt. Nothing normally fazed her. Something was very wrong. He watched as her mouth fell open and three words tumbled out.

"What the fuck?"

CHAPTER 22

"What the fuck?"

Rhiannon stared down in disbelief at the shredded book cover, its yellowed inner pages visible behind heavily carved letters. She was seething. "What have you done?"

Vince's jaw dropped in an almost comical expression of surprise. "Huh?"

"Why did you do that? What the hell were you thinking?"

"I don't know what you're talking about..."

She lifted the book and showed him. "It's a library book, nimrod. How do I take it back now? They'll charge me."

His furry unibrow furrowed in the middle. His eyes darkened. "It's nothing to do with me, you crazy bitch."

Rhiannon flinched at his insult. *How dare he.* She glared at the message he had left for her on the cover.

DON'T
LOOK
INSIDE

Yeah, right. She knew what Vince was getting at. He was telling her that she should grow up, that she was too old for children's books, that only little girls dressed like fairy tale princesses. In the early days of their relationship he would often compliment her on her individuality, sometimes even confess that he was attracted to her quirkiness. But he had changed. He was just like everybody else now.

To hell with him, she thought. *He can't tell me how to live my life.*

She ripped open the book.

She flipped past the first couple of pages to the beginning of the story. She sighed, annoyed with herself for getting angry. Never mind. She had her new favorite book to take her mind off it all. *Cat's Curiosity.* She'd lose herself in its verses and forget her troubles soon enough.

Stop! Gwen Johnson's only daughter
Turn back now, avoid your slaughter.
Continue on to the regatta
And there'll be no happily ever after.

Rhiannon sat there in open-mouthed shock for a few moments. How had he done that? She glanced over at the accompanying illustration and saw what looked like Vince's car, a rusty Austin Princess, driving along an empty country road. There were two occupants inside. She leaned closer. They looked awfully like Rhiannon Johnson and Vincent Wade.

Her stomach filled with rocks. She loved Vince, but he didn't have an artistic bone in his body. This was not his doing. There was something else going on here.

People were always telling her that she was out of touch with reality - had she now tipped completely into her own fantasy world? Normally she could tell the difference between her daydreams and real life, but this...

She blinked and looked again. The words and the illustration were still there.

Ear-shattering death metal blasted from the car stereo and suddenly she couldn't stand it. She reached over and pressed the eject button.

"Hey!" Vince yelled. "What the hell?"

Rhiannon stared at the cassette hanging from the mouth of the machine and couldn't help but think that it looked like the stereo was blowing her a raspberry. "Who did you tell?" she asked calmly.

"Put the tape back in."

She grabbed the cassette and threw it over her shoulder. She heard it clatter into the rear footwell. "Who did you tell?" she repeated, the volume of her voice rising. "About what we're doing today?"

He blinked hard. "Are you nuts?"

"Apparently."

"Seriously, what are you saying?"

"Who knows about the plan?"

"Us. You and me. Jesus…"

"Who else?"

"Nobody else, you crazy bitch."

She felt her cheeks flush red. If he called her a crazy bitch one more time she'd rip his head off and spit down his neck.

She pushed the open book into his face. "Well, somebody sure as hell knows!"

Vince struggled to see out of the windshield. The car swerved. He batted the book away. "What are you doing? I'm driving!"

Rhiannon took the book back. This was all Vince's doing, it had to be. A bad joke that he was starting to regret, maybe, or a test…

Yes. That was it. He was testing her loyalty. Checking to see if she would go through with it. He'd always had major trust issues.

Something caught her eye in the passenger side mirror. She peered into the reflection and gasped. There was somebody behind her, in the back seat.

A woman.

Her heart lurched. She spun around.

The back seat was empty. She turned back and checked the side-view mirror again. Nothing.

Great. Now she was seeing things. Maybe this really was all just in her head. She glanced down at the page and continued reading.

You like to play the innocent card
Sweet Rhiannon, emotionally scarred
In truth you are sharp as a tack
His crimes are an aphrodisiac.

Your handsome prince is a dangerous toad
Your carriage a rust heap, unfit for the road.
You know the sky's not made of toffee
Wake up and smell the fucking coffee.

She looked up slowly, staring ahead. "I want out."
"What?"
"Stop the car."
"Rhiannon…"
"Stop the car!"
Vince growled with fury. His foot pressed down on the gas. "No, it's too late for that. There's no turning back, do you understand?"
But Rhiannon wasn't listening. Her eyes were fixed on something in the field up ahead. The figure of a woman in a nightgown, standing perfectly still in the long grass, watching them. Rhiannon stared back as they passed. The strange woman never took her eyes from the car, smoothly rotating in an eerily unnatural manner until Rhiannon was watching her through the rear window.

She turned to Vince. "Did you see that?"

He rolled his eyes. "See what? Another magical water tower? I'm trying to drive here, you crazy -"

"Crazy what? Go on, say it. Say it one more time."

"Or what? You'll leave me? You think you'll find someone else? Just look at you. Take a good look at yourself, princess."

He reached over and pulled down her sun visor. She peered up into the small mirror and saw her eyes well up.

She also saw, through the film of tears that blurred her vision, a woman grinning at her from the back seat of the car.

It was the woman from the field, only now Rhiannon could see that her face was peeling off at the hairline to reveal the underlying skull. Her neck was a tangle of rotting sinew. As her grin widened large chunks of flesh crumbled away from her cheeks.

Rhiannon screamed.

Vince grimaced and put a hand to his ear. "What the hell is wrong now?"

"Look behind you!"

"What?"

"The back seat!"

Vince huffed and checked the rearview mirror. "There's nothing, okay? Get a grip."

"Listen to me, mister man." Her voice shook. She collected herself for a moment. "I don't care what you think. I can't handle this anymore and I need to get out."

Rhiannon's trembling hands grabbed at the handle of the passenger door. It was locked. She tried again anyway. She yelled in frustration, pulling at her hair. "Please, Vince, please. Just stop the fucking car."

He rolled his eyes and looked away. She lurched over and grabbed the steering wheel.

"No!" Vince yelled. The car swerved dangerously. He prized her fingers off the wheel and pushed her back into her seat. "You're crazy. You're one crazy bitch, you know that?"

Rhiannon fumed. Her upper lip twitched and her cheeks turned purple. It was only her fear of what was behind her that stopped her from launching at him. She spoke through gritted teeth. "Look. Behind. You." Maybe the gruesome dead woman would do all the dirty work for her.

"Okay," Vince shouted. "Okay, fine. You want me to look? You want me to turn around and risk our lives while driving and take a good look? Then I will."

He turned, and looked.

The rear seat was empty save for more of Rhiannon's library books. "Happy now?"

He turned back to face front.

A woman stood in the road directly ahead of them.

A woman in a nightgown.

Vince slammed on the brakes. "Shiiit—"

The car barreled toward her.

Rhiannon screamed.

With only moments until impact, the woman sprung into the air and launched at the car. Her hideous, grinning face hurtled toward them. Rhiannon and Vince braced themselves.

Rhiannon hid behind her hands.

An almighty thump as something hit the hood of the car.

Rhiannon peeked between her fingers. The last thing she ever saw was Miriam's cracked visage pressed up against the windshield.

CHAPTER 23

Della slid into the driver's seat of Graham's patrol car and slammed the door. A fine mist of sweat glazed her brow. She had found Gwen's apartment cramped and confining, but even out on the landings and stairwells she had felt a crushing sense of claustrophobia. She eased her neck back until it was cushioned by the headrest and closed her eyes. Her own darkness was comforting, despite the persistent pounding in her skull.

"Come on, then," Graham said, as he climbed into the passenger seat, his gruff voice sawing through her brain. "Now it's your turn."

She groaned. Kept her eyes closed. "What?" She knew exactly where this was headed, but the tremor in her voice surprised her anyway.

"Spill the beans. Why did you leave the good ol' US of A to come to this freaky sludge pile of a town?"

She couldn't help but chuckle. Her eyes opened with a heavy reluctance. She started the engine and reversed out of the space. Threw the vehicle into gear and peeled out of the lot.

Della turned and looked into Graham's craggy face, with its intriguingly crooked features. She saw the pain in his eyes that had drawn her to him initially, that had made him feel like a kindred spirit, somehow. She wasn't sure if it was because she felt obliged to reciprocate, given that he had earlier opened his own heart to her, or because she had a burning desire to tell *someone*, but as she drove through the center of town and out into the countryside, she found herself telling him everything.

***

Breathe.

Della checked her firearm. Her mouth was dry.

She had never fired her weapon outside of a training scenario, a fact of which she had always been immensely proud. But right now, on the landing directly outside Virgil Durand's apartment, that fact inspired nothing but fear.

The fingers wrapped around her gun shook with adrenalin, so she compensated by clasping the weapon tighter. She grabbed her wrist with her other hand to steady herself. In her former life she would have been home by now, safe and warm with dinner on the stove and a good book in her hands.

But no. You wanted more.

She had grown tired of patrolling the Fenway Park area, dealing with the same assholes, drunks, and over-excited baseball fans, and she desired something else. She wanted - she needed - that *rush.*

Well, you got it.

She had recently been made detective in Special Investigations, a unit that dealt with vice crimes and drug activity, specifically targeted to street level dealers and users. Virgil Durand had been on their radar for some time, and following a tip-off they had been given the go-ahead to raid his apartment.

Della glanced up at her partner, Mike, poised at the other side of the door. He shot back a smile that was too nervous to be reassuring.

A mom and her two kids exited an apartment farther down the corridor. The mom made eye contact with Della and froze.

Della's stare hardened. She subtly shook her head. The woman ushered her children back inside and closed the door.

Mike held out three fingers, then two. His head nodded with the rhythm of his count. Della steeled herself.

She mouthed 'one', and Mike kicked the door down.

***

Virgil Durand, it turned out, was not at home that afternoon, but a sickly sweet smell led Della and Mike to one of the bedrooms where they made an interesting discovery.

The humidity hit Della as she entered the room, her shirt clinging to her back as if sucked there, her skin instantly wet. Condensation dripped onto her from the ceiling, where a series of long chains hung. At the end of these chains were strip lights wrapped in aluminum foil, suspended only a few feet from the floor, beneath which stood young plants in trays of water. Paper ducts coiled around each of the lights, snaking up to holes in the ceiling.

Della had never seen a cannabis factory before - she had mostly dealt with harder drugs, specifically crack cocaine, in her short time with the unit - and she found it quite fascinating. Her eyes followed the cables that ran in knots from the strip lights to an extension socket, and what she saw on the floor made her heart leap. Condensation was dripping onto the electrics, causing water to pool around the cables.

"We need to call the electricity board," Mike said, just as the words were about to leave her lips.

Almost one hour later, with the electricity turned off and the room safe, Della pulled out a camera and proceeded to catalog their haul. Mike peeled the baking foil away from the windows to let in some light, but by that time it was getting dark outside. They collected evidence by flashlight, taking samples of different sized plants and placing them into paper bags marked with exhibit labels.

Della scanned the room with her flashlight to assess the size of the job.

"I know," Mike said. "This is gonna take a while."

"I think we'll need to call for extra man—"

She halted mid-thought. Her flashlight beam had hit something.

A leg.

Someone was there. Across the room.

Fear paralyzed her for a moment. She raised the beam.

A bearded man in a heavy jacket, squinting in the glow. She recognized him from his mugshot on file.

Virgil Durand.

She jumped, dropping the flashlight.

"Mike…" she whispered.

She reached down, her hands shaking as she pulled the firearm from its holster. She scrambled on the floor for the flashlight, grabbed it, holding it tight to the barrel.

Raised the gun.

Glanced over at Mike. He was rooted to the spot, staring at the other side of the room, his mouth agape. His gun holstered.

She was on her own.

Her head snapped forward. The beam of the flashlight searched for a moment, then found Durand again.

This time the barrel of a twelve-gauge shotgun stared her down.

For one awful moment she couldn't find her voice. "Drop your weapon," she ordered. "Now!"

Silence. Durand remained horribly still.

If he fired, it was over. She'd be blown to pieces.

"Do it!"

She had an advantage, she figured. She could see him, and he was blinded by the beam. But he had a shotgun. One blast in the general direction of her flashlight's glow would be enough.

She had no choice. She had to disarm the threat.

"This is your last chance."

Durand stood his ground. Steadied the shotgun against the side of his body and raised the barrel slightly. Ready to shoot.

She aimed for his shoulder and fired.

Even with the gun blast ringing in her ears Della heard the crash as Durand fell onto one of the strip lights. She stumbled through the dark, following the sound of the swinging chains as they creaked to a stop. She listened for Durand's groans, but heard none, her veins filling with ice in the eerie silence. She swept her flashlight in an arc until the beam found him, splayed out on the floor.

"No…"

His neck was shredded. An ever-expanding dark slick had formed around his upper body. The pool hit Della's boots. She crouched beside him.

His eyes were glassy. Lifeless.

"Mike…" she called.

She had missed Durand's shoulder, that was all too clear. Had her aim been off? Was it the glare from the flashlight? Had he moved at the last second?

Oh, Christ.

"Mike, Mike, I think he's…"

The thump of footsteps coming from outside the room. She raised her flashlight. Her heart in her mouth.

The door flew open.

Two children burst in. A boy of around five, a girl of three.

"Dad?"

"Daddy…"

The boy stopped in his tracks as he saw the body on the floor.

The girl kept coming. Her feet skated in the puddle as she approached her father, and she went down. She scrambled to her knees, her white dress and half her face thick with blood.

"My daddy…" She cradled his head in her tiny lap. "My daddy, my daddy…"

The boy's face was frozen in a mask of horror. His wide eyes flicked from his father to Della.

His chin wobbled. "What have you done?"

Della felt helpless in his gaze. "I'm sorry…"

"What have you done?" The pitch of his voice rose to a scream. "What have you done to my dad?"

He crumpled to his knees, sobbing. His sister began to howl. Della watched on, the anguish of the children tearing her apart.

"Help," the little girl cried, staring into her father's dead eyes. "Please help."

There was nothing Della could do.

***

Della paused her story as she navigated the winding hillside, the road narrowing, its surface becoming more uneven as she descended. She steered through a tight bend and peered over the road barrier at the steep drop below, imagining just how terrifying it would have been if Graham were driving right now and she was in the passenger seat, holding on for dear life.

"How far to go?"

"We're almost there," Graham said. "Anyway, you were saying…"

Della sighed. "Yeah." Recounting the story had dragged up all the old emotions, and the thought of continuing exhausted her. "So I was suspended for a few months, pending an investigation. And, well, you know how it is. A few months turned into a year, and during that time they sent me to see a police psychologist because I was still pretty torn up about what had happened. But it was my partner Mike's testimony that allowed me to keep my job, and by then I was itching to get back. So I turned up that first day, and the captain called me into his office - and he passed my gun back across the desk."

She sucked in a quick breath. "That's what did it. I couldn't even bring myself to pick up the weapon, so I knew it was over. I was finished. But I still loved the job. That's what made me think of England."

"No guns?"

"Right. Law enforcement at a slower pace. Less chance of - well, I just knew that if I ever got into that situation again, where I had to - you know..." She trailed off. "It would be the end of me."

Graham nodded. He turned his attention back to the road. Saw something up ahead, craning his neck. "Oh dear. Looks like they never made it to the regatta, after all."

Della followed his line of sight. What she saw stirred the panic in her belly, and that in turn caused an aching in the back of her throat.

She eased up on the gas pedal, bringing the car to a stop. She opened the door and swung her legs out, her manner calm, professional and efficient. *Let's get this done.*

Inside she wished she could be anywhere else in the world.

CHAPTER 24

Fireworks exploded in the darkening sky high above the crashed Austin Princess. The car jutted out of the hillside, its outer shell intact save for the wedge-shaped front end, the hood concertinaed against the unforgiving wall of earth and chalk. Chunks of broken headlamp decorated the road, sparkling like cat's eyes as another bursting rocket lit up the heavens.

Della had attended enough fatal road accidents in her career to know that, given the state of the vehicle, she would expect to find survivors. Bloody, perhaps, but alive. Her gut, however, told her that things would be different this time.

Nonetheless, the gruesome sight that greeted her when she peered in through the shattered side window still shocked her.

They were upright in their seats, heads back, eyes locked forever on the swirling yellow smoke stains ingrained into the fabric that padded the roof.

Identical hang-rope tattoos circled their necks.

"She was here," Graham said, surveying the scene from the opposite window.

Della nodded. A voice in her head reprimanded her for agreeing with him so readily. "Somebody was," she said. "Somebody was, that's for sure."

She glanced up from the burn marks, her vision resting on the balls of ice that had until recently been the girl's eyes. Della yearned, in that moment, for a job where she no longer had to look upon the faces of the dead.

She heard Gwen's coarse voice in her mind. *Promise me.*

She flinched. Pulled her head out of the car.

She felt sick.

Graham nudged past her. He grumbled a quick apology and poked his head through the window. Della didn't care what he was up to. She wanted out of there. She stumbled away, toward the back of the car. Her forehead pulsed, pushing down on her brow, like the worst migraines always did.

The world swam. She grimaced, dropping her head, cupping it in her hands.

Afterimages of the dead girl remained.

***

Graham saw pages splayed, on the seat beneath the folds of Rhiannon's dress. He reached for the book, his hand knocking it shut. He saw the cover and growled. Not the one. He peered through the darkness of the vehicle. Books littered the back seat.

He opened the passenger door. The dome light came on, illuminating the bodies, casting its sickly orange glow over them. He almost expected them to jolt to life, like a pair of grotesque puppets in a carnival booth.

More books in the footwell. He rifled through them. Lifted the dead girl's feet and checked the book he found under her pink slippers.

No. He stood, glanced back down, and gasped.

There. On the top of the pile.

He'd discounted it on first glance. It had looked so… ordinary. The embossed illustration was less prominent than he remembered, and the color of the leather had faded with age, but there was no doubting it, this time.

He'd found it.

He reached down, his heart slamming in his chest, and picked up the book.

Della rubbed her eyes and lifted her head, her vision clearing of stars. The first thing she saw was the crashed vehicle's trunk, oddly illuminated by a shaft of moonlight on the otherwise dark road.

The trunk jutted out from the car at a sharp angle, following the line of the rear window and giving the false appearance of a hatchback. The trunk itself was relatively small, with areas of peeled paintwork, and a pattern of heavy scratches around the rusting release button.

Della felt a sudden and powerful urge to look inside.

The brief flash of a fleeting firework was enough for Graham to read the spine: *Cat's Curiosity*, by Bertrand Powell. His hands trembled. He couldn't quite believe it: the book was back in his possession after all these years.

He examined the cracked leather of the front cover. The devilish, smirking child glared out from her prison of branches, her gleaming oval eyes appearing, in one swift, darting motion, to fix on him, her stare unbroken, even as Graham tilted the book away toward the dim light emanating from the vehicle.

Effective optical illusion, he thought. They really knew how to make creepy-looking books in those days. He managed a wry smile, but behind it the fear was already beginning to fog his mind, and his chin wobbled uncontrollably.

Miriam...

A violent tearing sound.

A guttural cry escaped his lips. It was happening.

A deep gash appeared in the leather.

His body stiffened, his fingers clamped tight around the book. He watched, mouth agape, his eyes filling with awed tears, as those familiar words scratched into the dark material.

DON'T
LOOK
INSIDE

Della stared at the trunk of the car, her finger poised over the release button. She had a hunch that this was something she simply had to do, and she had learned never to ignore her hunches, but there was something niggling at her.

She didn't feel in control.

Something was telling her that she needed to open the trunk. And yet those tangles of fear were present in her belly, reminding her of the hatch in the cell door, and April's cold little hands grabbing at her wrists, and those words, those three whispered words...

DON'T
LOOK
INSIDE

Graham studied the warning. Flaps of shredded leather fluttered in the breeze.

His thumb wrapped itself around the edge of the cover.

WAIT!

He tried to force his fingers to resist, but the message never left his brain. It was no use. He was no longer in control of his actions. The book turned in his hand and he watched, mystified, as if playing no part in its movement.

"Stop," he whispered. "Please…"

Even as the words left his mouth he was overcome with a hideous compulsion to *know.* Wasn't it time? Hadn't he wondered, every night for the past twenty-two years, exactly what *had* been inside?

No. He had resisted this urge before. He could do it again. What had changed?

As the cover parted a little, revealing the edges of the yellowed pages beneath, he thought he knew.

The desire to look inside was stronger now. She had been working on it. Now she was ready.

Ready for him.

Graham gritted his teeth, letting slip an exasperated moan of defeat.

He could only watch.

DON'T
LOOK
INSIDE

Here goes, Della thought. She popped the release button.

The trunk sprang open.

CHAPTER 25

Della emerged from the back of the car to find Graham slumped against the hood of the vehicle. He was so engrossed in a book that he didn't notice her.

Della recognized the embossed leather of the book cover immediately.

"Hey, you found it!"

Graham jumped. He slammed the book shut.

Della saw now, as she stepped closer, that there was something terribly wrong. Graham's face was twisted with a look of such undiluted horror that it rooted her to the spot.

"Graham…?"

He tried to speak. A gurgled moan was all that escaped his lips.

"Graham, Christ, what is it? What's wrong?"

He looked up slowly, but not enough to meet her eye. She saw the anguish etched into his weathered features. Tear tracks disappeared into the craggy folds of his cheeks.

"I -" His breath hitched. "I have to end it."

He reached into his jacket.

Della's eyes widened. "What...what are you doing?"

He grabbed something from his inside pocket. Pulled it out.

"Stop! Wait -"

A lighter. He snapped it open. Held the book up to the flame.

"No!" Della dived for the book.

Graham jumped up and turned away, holding it out of her reach.

"Don't..."

She ran around, grappling for it.

His fist shot out, slamming into the side of her face.

She recoiled, clutching her cheekbone.

Bastard. He punched me.

She leapt onto his back and swung her arm, batting the lighter out of his hand. It clattered to the ground. She made a grab for the book.

He bucked. Spun her. Thrust out an elbow, hurling her off. She crashed into the open passenger door and collapsed to her knees. The impact winded her. She gasped for breath.

Graham scrambled on the tarmac, searching for the lighter. "I should have destroyed it all those years ago. When I had the chance." He checked beneath the vehicle. "I can't make the same mistake again."

"It's evidence," Della said, between gulps of air. "Our only evidence. In a multiple homicide case."

He turned back to her. "You really don't get it, do you? This whole thing - it's the book. We get rid of the book, we get rid of her."

He caught sight of the lighter beneath the front tire. Reached down for it, dropping the book.

Della seized her chance.

Graham picked up the lighter and turned back, just as Della's hand closed around the book.

He growled, launching a fist that connected under Della's chin, jolting her jaw, smashing her teeth together.

The force of the punch drove her backward, into the road. She sprawled out, ripples of pain penetrating her skull.

She winced, sucking the sharp night air through her teeth. This fight was really not helping her headache.

She blinked hard, peering up at the night sky. Seeing double. As the two images merged into one, pinpricks of light streaked across her vision, creating the illusion of shooting stars.

She registered the familiar constellations. Found it odd that the night sky should look the same here as it did back in Boston. It struck her that there was something terrible about that. As if the world was telling her that she was already home. That Chalkstone was home now.

Graham retrieved the book.

Della sprang back up, battling through her wooziness. Her fury propelled her on.

She snapped at the book like an angry dog, tearing it from Graham's grasp. The stunned expression on his face delighted her.

She held the book aloft. "No such thing as ghosts, you old fool." She brought it down in a sweeping arc, cracking him across the side of the head.

He dropped to the asphalt, clutching his face.

"You bitch!" he screamed, his eyes watering. "You broke my nose!"

She opened her coat, looking for somewhere to stash the book.

He was back up, charging her. She held out an arm to block him, but his hands clamped tight onto the book.

She yanked it from his grip for a moment. He was back on it immediately. Blood trickled from his nose as he pulled.

Della grimaced, refusing to let go. The thought crossed her mind that she could sink her teeth into his arm, but that seemed uncouth. Especially given that she had just bust his nose. She felt kinda bad about that. Although given his already crooked features, a lopsided nose would probably fit right in.

Graham put his weight behind the book. With one swift pull he snatched it from her.

Della yelled in frustration. She pounced for it again.

She registered the look of open-mouthed shock on Graham's face.

His hands were empty.

She scanned the ground for the book. Looked across the road.

It was dancing in the breeze, flipping over and over, its pages splayed like wings, giving it purchase on the air.

It hit the road barrier with a reverberating clang and somersaulted up and over, dropping out of sight.

She met Graham's eyes.

"It's better off gone," he said. "Just leave it."

To hell with that. She had missed her vacation for this case. She wasn't going to give up that easily.

She bolted across the road and leapt the barrier.

Graham called after her. "What are you doing? Be careful -"

The earth on the other side was more uneven than she had anticipated. She stumbled, falling to one knee in a tangle of brambles. The ground fell away quite steeply only a footstep away. She peered over the edge. The hillside was muddy and thick with shrubs. Beyond that she saw the riverbank, a bench, an outbuilding. A busted old rowing boat in the water.

No book.

She steadied herself, holding out her arms for balance. Hesitated a moment before tottering down the hillside, her feet moving fast to keep up as she gained speed. She slowed as the bank leveled out.

She came to a stop, her shoes squelching in mud. Scanned the area. Nothing.

She saw the lights of the regatta in the distance. A streak of beaming light soared into the sky, exploding in a shower of sparks that illuminated the riverbank.

A figure, thirty feet away. Silhouetted against the momentarily bright sky. Watching her.

A woman.

Della headed in her direction. "Hey!"

The woman remained perfectly still.

Della marched on.

She stumbled, her feet sinking deep into the sticky mud.

She looked back up. The figure was gone.

She glanced around. Saw no-one. Headed to the platformed area where the figure had been. A drain. She stepped onto it.

The book was beneath her, at the exact spot where the figure had stood, its pages spiraling rapidly in the breeze.

A crazy thought struck her.

The woman. Could it have been…?

The book distracted her. She knelt over it. As the pages turned, she was consumed with a feeling of dread.

This was very wrong.

The verses and illustrations she had seen earlier in the day were now gone, replaced by what, at first, she mistook for blank pages.

No. Something was written there, in the center of every page. Repeated over and over, in the same shaky handwriting.

She leaned closer.

Two words.

Two words that caused her world to tilt on its axis. She clamped a hand over her mouth.

Her eyes welled with tears as she considered the implications of what she had just read.

"Della!" Graham's voice. Distant.

She scooped up the book. Held it to her chest.

She twisted around, looking up. Scanned the length of the road barrier. It was too dark. She couldn't see him.

"Are you okay?" he called.

"It's..." Her voice cracked. She cleared her throat. Tried again. "It's gone," she responded. "In the river."

A pause. "Let's get back."

"Coming."

She looked down at the open page before her, trembling.

Flicked through the book. Studied each identical page.

The same two words.

HE LIED

CHAPTER 26

She let Graham drive them back because she wasn't feeling up to it. They journeyed in silence, which suited Della just fine. If he had tried to engage her in conversation she knew there was a good chance that she would have performed a Graham Special and puked all over the dash.

Graham parked the patrol car behind the station. Della climbed out, struggling as she hoisted the heavy black canvas backpack onto her shoulder.

"Let me get that," he said.

"It's fine," she snapped. She offered a weak smile by way of an apology. He looked ridiculous standing there, two balls of blood-stained tissue plugging up his nostrils. At any other time, Della would have found it amusing.

They walked together, through the rear entrance, along the east corridor. Graham did his best to slow to her pace. They entered the locker room.

Della eased the bag off her shoulder and placed it carefully onto the bench. She stretched her back and groaned. Opened her locker and pretended to sort the contents, watching out the corner of her eye as Graham collected his things. She dawdled as he hung up his coat and switched to his motorcycle jacket. Grabbed his helmet. Locked up.

He passed her. Nodded. "Night."

She smiled. Nodded back. "Goodnight."

Della waited, her breath quickening.

She listened. Graham's footsteps retreating down the corridor. The creak of the rear entrance doors as they swung shut behind him.

Della reached into her jacket and pulled out the book.

She ran her fingers over the raised apples and imitation tree bark that made up the frame of the cover. Studied the girl in the center of the illustration, thick branches growing from her head like grotesquely oversized antlers.

The image shocked her, as if she was seeing it for the first time. Not because of the sinister grin plastered on the girl's face, nor the glint in her eyes that hinted at a uniquely malicious kind of mischief, but because Della detected something else, hidden away, behind the gruesome visage.

A cry for help.

It chilled Della to look upon her. Images of Virgil Durand's bloodied children forced their way into her mind, that awful mixture of horror and disbelief etched onto their faces, a desperate panic in their eyes. Begging for someone to save their dying father...

She flinched.

Placed her thumb on the corner of the cover, ready to open the book. She hesitated.

A small puncture hole appeared in the top left of the cover.

The rip expanded downward in a line.

Della staggered back.

It was happening.

Screeee—screeee—screeee—screeee—

Her first thought was that the squeal was emanating from the book somehow, but then her head snapped up.

No...

The alarm grew louder.

Her heart sank as she realized that, once again, she was the only person left in the station.

Just leave it.

She had no choice.

You promised you'd ignore it next time.

She had to go.

She returned her attention to the book.

The rip in the leather had vanished.

***

Della opened the door to the cell block, the book tight in her grip, and stepped into the darkness. A rush of cold air hit her immediately.

SCREEEE—SCREEEE—SCREEEE—SCREEEE—

She groped around for the light switch, her fingers finding a cobweb instead. She cringed, wiping it against the crumbling brickwork just as the door slammed behind her, cutting out the remaining light.

A rush of panic. She touched her belt.

Her keycard was there. She reprimanded herself for not remembering to check first.

She fumbled for the light switch and flipped it. A delay, as usual.

She stared, wide-eyed, into the darkness. That abysmal Chalkstone darkness: a void that seemed to look inside you if you dared peer into it for too long.

Her head throbbed in time with the excruciating squeal of the alarm.

The lights blinked.

In that brief flash she saw everything she would normally expect to see - the custody desk, the gray walls, the noticeboard, the speckled linoleum, the door to the exercise yard - and something else.

The shape of a person.

Standing ahead of the desk. Watching her.

Pitch black again.

Her heart leapt.

A trick of the mind, she reasoned. *When the lights come back on, I'll see it for what it really is.*

A second blink of illumination. The figure was much closer now. Halfway between Della and the custody desk. An impossible distance to cover in the time that had elapsed between flashes.

A woman. Staring at her through a parting in her long red hair.

The same woman she had seen briefly at the riverbank.

The lights flicked off, plunging Della back into darkness.

It can't be.

Definitely not her imagination that time. A powerful wave of fear rippled through her body.

Miriam?

She heard shuffling in the dark. Bare feet on linoleum, perhaps. Was the woman edging toward her?

She tried to take a step back but couldn't. She wanted nothing more than to turn and get the hell out of there. But the fear had paralyzed her.

Another flicker of light. A shorter burst than the others.

Miriam was there. A foot away. In her face.

Della screamed.

Back to black.

An afterimage remained of the hideous visage.

Gray. Rotting. Twisted with rage.

Della heard her own sobs. Her lip quivered. She tried to pull herself together.

The lights fizzed, then sparked to life. They stayed on this time.

Della was frozen to the spot. She saw only the empty cell block.

Whatever had been there was gone.

She fell back against the door, her breath escaping in long, panting gasps.

I'm not crazy, she told herself. *That was real.*

SCREEEE—SCREEEE—SCREEEE—SCREEEE—

A twist in her stomach. She still had a job to do.

If she was quick, she'd be done and out of there in thirty seconds.

She steeled herself.

Made a run for it.

She dashed to the custody desk and scooted behind it. Scoured the control panel. In her haste she couldn't find what she was looking for.

"Come on, come on..."

Got it. She turned the key.

SCREEEE—

Silence.

She exhaled.

The rhythm of the alarm continued as a pulsing in her temples.

She chanced a look down the cell corridor.

Something stood there, she was sure of it. Enveloped in darkness at the far end. A figure.

Forget it. It's nothing.

She navigated around the desk. Glanced up at the exit.

Run.

She bolted, like a sprinter off the blocks.

Almost immediately she tripped over her own feet and lost her balance. She crashed to the ground, the book falling from her grasp and skating along the linoleum.

She groaned. The floor was a blanket of grime-coated ice on her cheek. She looked up. The book was ahead of her. She stretched out an arm but couldn't reach. She dragged herself up onto her elbows and knees and scuttled along, reaching out again. She grabbed the book this time and pulled it close.

Della's imagination conjured the words onto the cover moments before they actually appeared there, but it didn't lessen the shock for her when an invisible hand began to carve deep into the illustration. She recoiled, screaming.

The leather tore violently and quickly, the accompanying ripping noise causing Della to think of fingernails being wrenched from their beds. She watched, unable to fully comprehend what her eyes were showing her, as the image of the little girl was obliterated by a series of sharp slashes.

It was over in a matter of seconds. Della stared at the book and its newly-formed message in open-mouthed horror.

April and Graham were right. They had been right all along.

DON'T
LOOK
INSIDE

She cupped her head in her hands, rubbing her temples. Stared at the words through her fingers.

Reality had always been such a solid construct to her - she had built her entire belief system around its unshakable continuity - and in the last few seconds all of that had slipped away. Thank goodness for her headache and its constant, throbbing pain. Something to keep her anchored in reality as her world broke free of its moorings.

She grabbed the book and scrambled to her feet, her trembling legs only managing to carry her as far as the custody desk. She collapsed into a chair, refusing to look down the dark cell corridor to her left. She placed the book on the desktop.

She put her hand to the cover. Her fingers dipped into the indentations made by the letters.

She thought of the two words she had seen repeated in its pages by the riverside.

Despite the warning, her desire to open the book was intense and immediate. She simply had to know more.

This is insane.

Her thumb hovered over the corner of the cover.

The book pulsed.

She whipped her hand away.

Did that just happen?

She was certain that she had felt the book move beneath her palm, and she thought she saw the leather fluctuate, but... Sometimes her vision pulsed when her migraines got really bad.

She watched, unblinking.

Leaned closer.

Sure enough, the book was moving, the cover rising and falling in a careful rhythm, as if it was in fact a living, breathing creature.

She moved her hand back toward the book, slowly, hesitantly, as if appeasing an angry dog.

Rising, falling. Rising, falling.

In her mind she had a vision of the book as it sprang open, then immediately snapped shut again, like a bear trap, ensnaring her hands.

Her heartbeat was loud in her ears. To hell with the warning. She had to know what was inside.

The book stopped pulsing.

Della froze. Held her breath.

The air was heavy. Charged. Beneath everything she could hear that noise again. A living sound.

Before the rational part of her mind could tell her what a terrible decision she was making, Della tore open the book.

CHAPTER 27

Miriam paced the small square of garden that her husband had built for her the previous summer. She was impatient for him to return home, and had been unable to concentrate on any of her household chores all afternoon.

Her subconscious mind had decided to occupy itself with a game she had not played since childhood. *Step on a crack, break your mother's back* she chanted to herself, as she deftly avoided placing her foot on the gaps between the paving stones.

She heard the roar of a car engine, followed by its abrupt cessation, then the familiar whine of the garage door as it closed. Butterflies danced in her belly. She hopped between the slabs. *Step on a line, break your mother's spine.*

She saw him through the veil of white net curtains as he entered the house and she could tell, simply from the posture of his silhouette, that he was in a foul mood. Boy, did she have some news that would brighten his day.

"Graham," she called. "Out here."

After a few seconds his head appeared through the gap in the patio door. His eyebrows knotted. "What is it?"

"Take a seat." She motioned to the iron bench.

His eyes narrowed, suspicious. "Why?"

"Please, just sit down."

"I've got to get changed."

"This won't take a minute."

He huffed and marched over, throwing his weight onto the bench. Looked up at her.

She rubbed the backs of her hands. Smiled weakly. Now was her big moment, and she couldn't quite find the words. She met his gaze and her eyes filled with tears.

Graham's face softened. "Good God, woman, what is it?" He grabbed her hands and pulled her close.

She chuckled. "No, silly. They're happy tears. You see…"

He edged forward, his mouth falling open in expectation.

"…I'm pregnant."

His expression remained the same, except, Miriam noted, for one small detail. His eyes hardened.

Silence.

She laughed nervously, hoping his lack of response was just a comedic display of shock. "Well?"

He inhaled sharply, opening his mouth wider as if to speak, then said nothing.

Miriam waited. She looked down and noticed she was standing on a crack. She stepped away.

Graham rubbed the bristles on his chin. Ran a hand through his hair. "Are you sure?"

"Yes, I'm sure."

He nodded.

"I know it's not something we specifically discussed," she said, "but it just seems...right. Don't you think?"

His gaze slowly drifted to the floor.

"Graham?"

He blasted out a sigh and got to his feet.

Miriam moved to him, awaiting the inevitable embrace. Instead, Graham turned away from her and stepped into the house, disappearing behind the net curtains.

Miriam followed, entering just as a door slammed. He had hidden himself in his den. She wasn't going to let him get away with this. She stormed after him. As she entered the den he was hitting the TV remote on the arm of his chair, trying to get it to work. He threw it across the room.

"Graham," she said, trying to keep her anger in check, "we need to talk about this."

He picked up a newspaper and leafed through it. "I've had a rough day."

"I thought you had to get changed?"

"You're right, I do." He leapt to his feet. Marched to the doorway. "Excuse me."

She let him past. He stomped up the stairs. She called after him. "This is good news, though, right?"

He slowed to a stop. Backed up a few steps and turned to her.

He sighed deeply, the way she imagined he might when informing a family of the death of a loved one. "Look, I don't want to share you," he said. "With anyone."

He turned and retreated back up the stairs. Miriam had no comeback; his words had stunned her into silence.

I don't want to share you.

Well, it was too late for that.

That should have been her comeback, she realized now, but it was too late for that, as well.

His words rattled through her brain as she made her way through to the kitchen. She should have just let him brood for a while. Was this really what she wanted to hear? And what did it mean, anyway? She wasn't even going to entertain the idea of an abortion just because her husband was acting like a spoiled child.

She boiled the kettle for tea, as she always did on his return from work. It was something they did together, an evening ritual. She didn't care for the tea itself - with all the chalk clogging up the water pipes, there was no such thing as a good brew in this town - but it gave them an excuse to sit together, to chat about their day, and tonight they really needed to talk. She propped the kitchen door open so that he could hear the shrill whistle of the kettle, poured two cups, set them on the table, and waited. He'd be down soon for his tea, as he always was, and she would confront him.

He never came.

It remained that way for the next few weeks. She would corner him on his return from work, and he would slither away, uninterested. He didn't care that she was violently sick in the mornings, nor that she had started having strange dreams at night; dreams involving dead babies. That was all perfectly normal, she was sure; anxiety dreams were par for the course with the onset of motherhood, or so she had read in her baby books.

One night, however, everything changed. She awoke from a nightmare so vivid that it shook her to the core. What frightened her most of all was that her dream had the same feel as the visions she had experienced in her early teens - a series of psychic premonitions, all of which had come true. She turned to Graham, who was awake now, and cried words that caused dread to ripple across her flesh as she heard herself speaking them aloud: "The baby is going to die."

She didn't expect him to care; in her bleakest moments, she had even suspected that he hoped for that very thing. But his attentiveness surprised her. He flipped on the light, shocked by her outburst, and offered the embrace she had so longed for these past few weeks. He stroked her trembling arms and whispered soothing words into her ear. He pulled back from her, a reassuring smile brightening his face, and she saw the pure horror of what was to come reflected in his eyes.

His face fell. "What is it?"

She backed away. She could see only darkness in him.

Her premonitions continued throughout the pregnancy, progressing from night terrors to waking dreams, flashes of random images that made little sense but left no doubt as to their meaning. Whenever her husband tried to come to her aid Miriam became hysterical, screaming for him to keep away, for she could not bring herself to look upon him.

She began to believe that there was only one place the baby was safe, and that was inside her. Which made it particularly challenging for Graham on the night she went into labor. He had to force her into the car for the drive to the hospital, and the journey there was a demanding one, his wife thrashing about in the passenger seat, shattering the side window with her fist and screaming for him to stop and let her out.

Once in the delivery room it took two doctors and two orderlies to restrain her, and it was quickly decided that she should be sedated for the baby's safety. When she awoke hours later she was horrified to discover that it was all over and that the baby was out in the world - in the arms of her husband.

Her initial panic abated as she watched them together, Graham's obvious joy at being a father seeming to smooth his prematurely weathered features as he gazed upon his daughter swathed in blankets. All the darkness Miriam had previously seen in him was gone now, replaced with the Graham of old, a man she had always thought of as hangdog handsome. He suggested they name her Cherie, and Miriam's mind was too dizzy from the drugs for her to fight him. Cherie it was.

Her paranoia still rampant, Miriam refused to let the baby out of her sight, but staying awake was to prove an impossible task. She slept heavily and dreamt of chest freezers and axes and three little words (*don't look inside*) that meant nothing to her. A jumble of images that swirled in her unconscious mind until gradually they edited together to form a narrative that offered only one possible interpretation.

Her eyes flicked open. She finally knew how her baby would die.

She leapt from the bed and attacked Graham as Cherie lay asleep in her crib beside him. Miriam screamed hysterically, her hands and elbows everywhere, her jaws snapping at him like a rabid animal until Graham managed to grab her wrists and a nurse exploded into the room armed with a large syringe.

She was pricked to consciousness some time later by a tightening sensation around her wrists and ankles, but as soon as she realized she was being secured to the bed there was little she could do. She spat and cursed at the bored orderlies but the drugs had rendered her physically incapable of putting up any resistance. In the moments before she blacked out she heard a doctor explaining to Graham, in what she felt was an inappropriately jolly tone, that this sort of thing was surprisingly common following the trauma of pregnancy, and that she would most likely be committed to the ward for psychological evaluation.

When she next awoke, Cherie was gone. A nurse responding to her alarm calmly explained that her husband had taken the baby home. Miriam's hysterical cries could be heard throughout the entire wing of the hospital.

Three weeks later she was given the all-clear, and by that time the entire nine-month nightmare seemed like it had happened to someone else, her choppy premonitions easily dismissed as the product of wild pregnancy hormones.

Once outside the hospital she discovered that her husband was not waiting for her as she had expected; perhaps he had missed the message she'd left for him on the house phone. She hailed a taxi instead. The ride home was not something she would remember; she could only think of her daughter, and holding her in her arms for the first time.

As she arrived at the house the garage door was open, wide and black like a screaming mouth, daring her to enter. Her heart pounded in her chest as she stepped inside, navigating around Graham's mud-streaked Land Rover, and what she saw in the corner of the garage froze her blood solid.

A handwritten note on the chest freezer. Three words that had flashed before her eyes repeatedly during her premonitions, but that had not fully registered with her, until now.

don't look inside

The bags she was carrying dropped to the floor.

No. She ran into the house.

Everything was eerily quiet as she passed through the kitchen and into the hall. She found him in the dining room, rocking back and forth in the corner. Muttering something.

"Graham?"

He stopped moving and turned to her. He was dirty. Unshaven. His eyes were dead. She could see now that his clothes were covered in something. Panic rippled through her. It looked like blood.

"Graham, where's the baby?"

He mumbled something. She didn't catch it.

"Graham, where's the baby?"

"I never wanted to share you."

"What?"

"I did tell you that."

"What are you talking about?"

"The baby," he said, a runner of dribble hanging from his bottom lip. "The baby was a murderer."

"Just tell me, please. Where's Cherie?"

"You were fine, weren't you? We were fine. Until the baby came along. And that's when everything changed."

"Jesus Christ, Graham…what have you done?"

"The baby killed my wife."

"No, she didn't. I'm right here."

He squinted, as if seeing her for the first time. "Yes, you are. And at last we can be together again."

The horror of what must have happened hit her then. She turned and ran. She heard him call as she bolted down the hall. "Now it can be just the two of us…"

She exited into the garage, slowing as she approached the freezer. She put her hands to the lid, intending to get this over with quickly, but she lost her nerve. She couldn't do it. She stared at the message written in a shaky version of Graham's handwriting.

don't look inside

Her head was pounding. Her throat hurt. She exhaled in a long, shuddering breath and closed her eyes.

She lifted the lid and rested it against the crumbling brickwork of the garage wall. She opened her eyes and looked down.

Miriam came around on the concrete floor of the garage some time later. Vile images of the chest freezer's contents attempted to invade her mind, but she refused them entry. She exited the garage without looking around her, walking purposefully through the house and up the staircase. Once inside her bedroom she slipped off her shoes and unzipped her dress. She prepared for bed, removing her rings and necklace. Placed them in her jewelry box. She put on her white nightgown. Brushed her hair.

She found herself in the living room with no memory of how she got there, staring down at a book on the coffee table: *Cat's Curiosity* by Bertrand Powell. Cherie's book. She picked it up and leafed through it. Sniffed the pages, breathing in the stale aroma. She tidied the coffee table, straightened the net curtains, tied the noose.

She held the book tight to her as she climbed onto the iron bench in the garden and tightened the rope around her neck. When she leapt, the book clattered to the ground beneath her.

She hung from the beam for almost two days before the police came.

CHAPTER 28

Della crossed the quiet, tree-lined street, a respectable neighborhood of carefully manicured lawns and aging but well-preserved homes. She was drawn to one of the larger houses on the block. The garage door was open, beckoning her inside. From the road it looked like a gaping mouth, the second floor windows wide but lifeless eyes.

She moved down the driveway, stopping at the threshold of the garage, her heart thumping in her chest. It would have been sensible to call for back-up, but she knew this was something she had to do herself. It was personal now, the book had made it so. Besides, what assistance would she receive in this town? Okay, so in Boston she'd get a swarm of officers with Glocks, maybe even a full SWAT team, but in Chalkstone she'd be lucky if she got Kelvin - or was it Kevin? - with his nightstick. She hitched the heaving backpack onto her shoulder, took a deep breath and stepped inside.

She navigated around Graham's motorcycle, an enormous, black and chrome Harley that swallowed almost as much space in the garage as a small family car. Various tools hung from hooks on the back wall. She saw a shiny cabinet in the corner that seemed very unremarkable until it registered with her what it was. Her veins filled with ice.

The chest freezer. Still there after all these years. Incredible that he still owned it, or that he still lived in the house where it had all occurred, for that matter.

She edged forward, hypnotized by the metal box and the sickening thought of what it had once contained. Anyone else, guilty or not, would have packed up and moved on long ago. The fact that Graham had not was frightening to her. It was then that she realized she did not know the first thing about the man she was here to confront.

Graham knelt beside the mantel in the dining room, stoking a hungry fire that crackled in the grate. He watched the flames jitter and bop like demented hoofers on hell's dance floor, the occasional loud pop of the logs causing his eye to twitch. A single tear rolled down his leathery cheek as he placed the poker between the andirons.

In his other hand he fingered a gun.

He stared into the flames, his vision locked onto a single point, until his sight blurred and his mind traveled elsewhere. The book's hideous warning flashed before his eyes, accompanied by the acrid tang of the crashed car - a mix of gasoline and stale cigarette smoke - and suddenly he was back there, by the roadside, staring down at the carved words.

DON'T
LOOK
INSIDE

The hand that had opened the book seemed to do so against his will, as if he were a puppet with no control over his actions. The first page was yellowed and blank, save for two small words at the center, in faded type. He moved the book closer to read them. A dedication that chilled his bones.

For Daddy.

The sting of tears pricked his eyes. He blinked them away, his traitorous hand turning the page. He wanted nothing more than to look away but could not, as if an unseen force was both holding his head still and prying his eyes open.

A family portrait. Miriam, Graham, and a girl of around seven, huddled together on the floor of a photographer's studio, grinning for the camera. The smile on his face was not one he recognized. It seemed to belong to someone else, as if the version of Graham in the photo was a jolly doppelgänger.

Miriam looked stunning. A few years older than when he had last seen her alive but more beautiful than ever. And the angelic little redheaded girl was the spit of her mother...

His eyes snapped to the verses on the facing page.

> From birth I looked just like my Mom
> I even inherited her green thumb.
> But as for my future career
> When I looked to you my choice was clear.
>
> I wanted to make my Daddy proud
> For him to be there in the crowd.
> Watching as the brass band played
> During my passing out parade.
>
> Alas, this future remains unseen
> It's merely now what could have been.
> But we can all still be together.
> Come join us, Daddy - be ours forever.

Graham tumbled, his legs unable to support him. He fell back onto the hood of the car. His trembling fingers turned the page to one final image - a beautiful twenty-something woman in dress uniform, red curls spilling from beneath her cap as she saluted a senior officer.

He stared at the image until it began to tip and swirl, a wave of nausea rushing over him.

"Hey, you found it!"

Della. He slammed the book —

Graham jolted. Blinked. A white afterimage of flames remained, obscuring his vision. He put out a hand to steady himself and found the cold tile of the fireplace surround. His lips were dry and stuck together. He levered them apart with his tongue and lifted the gun. He screwed up his eyes and pushed the barrel into his mouth.

His breathing heavy, his heart beating in his ears, he winced at the taste of metal and gagged as the weapon pressed against the roof of his mouth. The book's images of his beautiful daughter flashed before him on a looping slideshow in his mind. He squeezed down on the trigger.

A muffled cry escaped his throat. *Wait.*

He opened his eyes.

This was why it had said *Don't Look Inside* on the cover of the book. This was exactly what *she* had wanted him to do. She'd waited all these years for him to look inside because she knew it would come to this. She'd predicted it. This was her end game.

No. He was not going to play into her hands. He eased off the trigger. Carefully removed the gun from his mouth and wiped his lips.

He hurled the weapon across the room. It bounced off the door jamb with a thundering crack.

Della stopped in her tracks and listened. The loud noise came from the room up ahead, at the end of the hall. She heard only the sound of her nervous panting. She held her breath. Stepped forward carefully, the book in one hand, her nightstick extended in the other. Turned and edged along the wall as she reached the doorway. Craned her neck around.

He was there, at the mantel, crouched down with his head in his hands.

She made her move. Pivoted around the doorpost and into the room.

Graham groaned, dragging his hands down his face. Della approached, silent. He opened his eyes. They widened as he saw her.

She froze.

His gaze dropped to something on the floor behind her. She looked back. A revolver.

He sprang forward, charging for it.

She dropped her nightstick, reached down and grabbed the gun, training it on him. "Don't move!"

He straightened, still on his knees. Raised his arms slowly in the air.

The gun shook in her hand. It was a snub nose revolver, considerably heavier than the Glock pistol she was familiar with. But the grip felt the same.

Virgil Durand flashed before her. She blinked him away.

"Don't move," she repeated, holding up the book. "Recognize this?" She threw it onto the dining table.

Graham's jaw tensed as he looked upon the book and suddenly he looked twenty years older. "You should have left it. Trust me, it was better off gone."

"It told me everything." Her voice trembled. "I know it was you, Graham. I know it was you all along, and not her."

"Don't believe a word," he said. "That's what she wants you to think."

"This whole time, it's you she's been after."

"No."

"You need to come with me. To the station."

"That's not going to happen."

"You're coming with me, Graham."

He shook his head. "You'll have to shoot me."

He closed his eyes, awaiting his execution.

Della held the weapon with both hands, attempting to steady herself, but she was trembling too much.

"Come on, then," he blasted, making her jump. He opened his eyes. "Do it! Put me out of my misery." He shuffled forward.

"Stop!" She pulled back the hammer.

He sighed. Clambered to his feet. "You're not going to do it, are you?"

"I said don't move, you son of a bitch."

He stepped forward. She took a step back.

He paused. Looked at her. His voice was calm now. "We both know you can't do this, Della."

"I'll do it, I'll shoot!"

"No, you won't. You won't, because you can't. Remember Durand. Remember what killing him did to you."

"Goddamn it, Graham. I don't want to shoot you, but I will. If I have to, I will."

"It destroyed you, didn't it? You can't do that again."

He lunged forward. Della screamed. He pressed his torso against the barrel. His face in hers.

"Now stop being silly," he said, "and put down the gun."

Her hand shook uncontrollably. His breath was hot and sour. Tears fell from her eyes. A cry hitched in her throat.

Graham placed a hand over hers and pushed gently away. "That's it. Good girl."

Della's body rocked as she sobbed. He stroked her face, wiping her tears. "Don't be upset. Come on." He cupped his other hand beneath the gun and removed it from her grip. "There."

He whipped the gun around and fired.

Della's chest exploded before she'd had a chance to register what had happened.

A high-pitched wheeze escaped her throat and she fell back against the wall, sliding down onto the floor, her head propped up against the baseboard. The shock on her face gave way to agony as a wave of excruciating pain rushed over her.

Her head toppled to one side as Graham loomed into view, expressionless. He pressed a boot into her chest until she was flat on the floor, staring up at the ceiling.

She realized now why the book had warned her: *Don't Look Inside.*

Miriam had known all along that if Della learned the truth, she would come here.

That this would happen.

Her eyes rolled back into her head until there was nothing but that awful Chalkstone darkness.

CHAPTER 29

Graham watched Della with a *told-you-so* look on his face as blood pumped from the corners of her mouth, running in rivulets down her neck and pooling around her collar. He sighed, wiping more of the red stuff from his boot. Part of him felt bad for the way things had worked out, but it was her stupid fault. She should never have come here. What was she thinking? He shook his head and turned away. Something on the table caught his eye.

The book. It was moving.

"What the f...?" He stepped closer. His jaw slackened at the incredible sight - the cover illustration had come to life. The little girl was swaying, her eyes bulging, her mouth widening into the kind of grin that he had seen before only on the faces of dangerous lunatics. He was drawn to her eyes that seemed inexplicably to glow, staring out at him from the cracked green leather. He leaned over the book, moving his head from side to side to make sure that her eyes were not following him, but what he saw instead caused him to spring back.

She winked.

The words came in a wave, so much faster than before, tearing up the leather and washing over the illustration, imprisoning the girl behind the slashed letters.

DON'T
LOOK
INSIDE

As his eyes focused on the warning he felt a presence. His stomach hardened. Something else was in the room, mere feet away, in the periphery of his vision. He was suddenly afraid to move. His eyes darted upward and there, standing in the doorway, was the rotting corpse of Miriam.

She looked unlike anything he had ever seen, her facial features a mangled mockery of beauty, her moldy gray skin cracked and split like the worn leather of the book cover. The blazing balls of fire that were her eyes rolled in their sockets and fixed on him. Her narrow lips stretched upward, tearing a crescent-shaped grin into her face. A set of razor-sharp cheekbones popped out, the membrane that covered them ripping open to reveal the gristle beneath.

She glided slowly into the room.

He fought the dizziness that had enveloped his mind and edged his way around the back of the table, crashing into a chair. She advanced in a straight line, as if on rails. He knew that if he stared into those eyes any longer he'd lose his sanity.

He pressed up against the wall, feeling the raised leaf pattern of the wallpaper against the palms of his hands. Miriam had decorated this room, he remembered then. Good job she'd done, too. He'd never had the patience for paper and paste.

The intense light in Miriam's eyes was hypnotic, but Graham forced himself to look away. He glanced down at the book. Those same eyes glowered back at him from between the carved letters. There was no escape from her penetrating glare.

Don't pick it up, he commanded his hands, but they shot out and grabbed the book anyway, lifting it from the table. It seemed somehow heavier than before, and as he watched a fine mist sprang out upon the surface of the cover, as if it was perspiring. The tome vibrated between his fingers with a pulsing rhythm, like the beating of a leather heart, and that was when he realized - the book was alive. It was a part of her, an extension of her - and much like the Miriam he had once loved, it held a magnetic allure that was impossible to resist.

DON'T
LOOK
INSIDE

He tried to look beyond the warning, as if avoiding the words would render them powerless. Miriam approached at the edge of his vision.

A hand that looked like his own but moved of its own volition brushed down the front of the book, over the embossed leaves and branches, the thumb hooking around the bottom of the cover and lifting it. He stared into the deep chasms of yellowed paper behind the carved letters and focused on a single point. Miriam was almost beside him now. If her dead hand reached out and grabbed him it was over. He would be hers. He concentrated hard, gritting his teeth, willing himself to do something.

His other hand twitched into life. It grabbed the book from the grasp of his demonic fingers and hurled it across the room.

The book fanned out in the air as it approached the mantel and landed with a satisfying *thunk* in the center of the fire.

Miriam instantly burst into flame.

Graham thought he registered a look of disbelief on her rotted face before her features contorted into a mask of agony, her mouth widening as she screamed, a silent howl that carried a faint echo to Graham's ears. He wasn't sure if it was delivered there by telepathy or his imagination, but it was blood curdling and terrible, and it brought a wicked smile to his lips.

Miriam's nightgown melted away like rice paper to reveal a pathetic charcoal skeleton. Her mouth continued to widen impossibly, beyond the limits of her jaw, yawning farther and farther back until it was a black hole that consumed her entire head. The flames retreated inward and rushed down, their rapid descent evaporating her bones from existence like the drop of a cloak at the finale of a magician's disappearing act.

The fire glowed unbearably bright, causing Graham to look away, and when he turned back a wisp of gray smoke was all that remained.

The book burned in the grate, claimed by the flames that licked around the cover. The pages curled and blackened. The little girl melted, her image warping. The distress etched onto her fast-expanding face suggested that she was feeling every moment of her fiery death.

Graham released a shuddering sigh and collapsed onto one of the dining room chairs. The last of the smoke dissipated around him.

He chuckled, but there was no levity in his voice as he spoke.

"Burn in hell, bitch."

CHAPTER 30

A humming noise punctured the silence. Della recognized the tune but she couldn't place it. She opened her eyes and saw only ceiling. A swirling pattern in the plaster. A light fitting with a dusty lilac shade. The silver strands of a cobweb.

Her body spasmed with pain. She clutched her chest and found only a jellied goo. Repulsed, she pulled her hand away. Her fingers were coated with thick red blood.

So this is dying.

What *was* that tune? She knew it. Better to concentrate on that than the pain. Where was it coming from?

As she gritted her teeth and braced against another wave of agony she suddenly realized that she no longer had a headache. The thought made her laugh, but no sound came out. Instead a torrent of blood gurgled up her throat and exploded out of her mouth like a serpent's tongue, before raining down on her face.

Shouldn't really laugh, she thought, almost laughing again.

The humming was louder now. *My Cherie Amour.* That was it! The old Stevie Wonder song. She turned her neck and saw Graham, kneeling by the fire, jabbing with a poker at what looked like a hunk of paper burning in the grate.

He glanced over and saw her. The humming stopped. He threw down the poker and got to his feet.

A pang of fear struck her belly and she welcomed it, marveling that it was possible to feel anything else beside the pain. Oh, to be a head in a jar right about now, entirely separated from her dying body.

Graham stood over her. She stared up at him. From her perspective it looked like he was wearing the lilac light shade as a hat. *That is not funny,* she told herself, very nearly laughing again. *Don't you dare find that funny.*

"Howdy," he said, affecting a bad American accent.

"What are you gonna do?" Della said, the force of getting the words out tearing her throat apart. "Chop me up and throw my pieces in the freezer?"

He sighed. Thought for a moment. "Sounds like a plan."

He reached down and grabbed her by the feet, dragging her across the carpet.

She screamed. The pain in her midriff was so immense that she felt as if at any moment her torso would tear apart below the ribcage, leaving Graham holding only her bottom half.

He pulled her through the doorway. Along the hall. Another lamp shade. More cobwebs. She had to do something to distract her mind from the shooting pain. She thought about Boston and Donna and the road trip. Where they would be right now. Where they were going.

All the sights whisking past the window - the mom and pop diners, the cheap motels...

Her head bounced as she was dragged through another doorway, the jagged metal tacks of the bare carpet gripper clawing into the soft flesh on the back of her skull.

...the offbeat roadside attractions, the craggy mountain summits. Swamps and rolling farmland...

Her scalp grated along the rough concrete of the garage floor. The dragging stopped. Graham threw her legs down. Searing pain coursed up her body. As her head rolled to one side she saw a blurry and bloody version of herself in a reflective surface. It was the shiny metal of the freezer casing.

As Graham turned away from Della his feet got caught up in something. He looked down. An empty black canvas backpack. Confused, he kicked it out of the way. He scanned the tool rack on the back wall of the garage and found what he was looking for. His hands clasped around the handle of an ax and pulled it from the rack. Brown stains of long-dried blood decorated the blade. He carried the weapon over to Della's body. Her face was contorted in a mask of agony as she writhed on the floor. "Never mind, my dear," he said. "It will soon be over."

He stopped in his tracks as he saw something on the chest freezer. He stiffened, goosebumps rippling his flesh. His head thumped. The world began to swim. He suddenly felt unsteady, the muscles in his legs trembling.

What the hell? He blinked several times as if to confirm what he was seeing was real.

A handwritten note, taped to the lid.

don't look inside

Della's words popped into his mind. *This whole time, it's you she's been after.*

No. Miriam was gone now, surely?

He stared at the words in disbelief, his mouth hanging open. He studied the torn and crumpled piece of lined notepaper. The feeling that overwhelmed him was one of rampant curiosity.

What is inside?

His hands were drawn to the cabinet. Once again he felt as if he had lost control of his limbs. His fingers clamped onto the lid.

His mind screamed.

No!

A smile formed on Della's lips. Her mind raced back to the scene of the car crash. Her finger pressing the release button on the back of Vince's car. The trunk springing open...

Inside she found a black canvas backpack. Curious, she unzipped it and threw back the flap. She gasped, covering her mouth with her hands.

DON'T

Graham studied the three terrible words that had haunted him for the past two decades. He watched, helpless, as his fingers wrapped around the edge of the lid. The curiosity of what was inside burned within him. He tried to resist but he couldn't help himself. The desire was too strong. His hands pulled up.

The lid cracked open.

LOOK

Della peered inside the backpack in the trunk. Four blocks, roughly the size and shape of house bricks. *Demolition Block M3A1* stamped on them. *Extremely hazardous.* Wires protruded from each block, leading to a plated central hub.

INSIDE

Graham threw the freezer cover wide open. The wire attached to the lid snapped. Horror dawned on his face as he peered down into its contents. A sharp gasp of realization formed his last breath.

Della's grin widened. She was laughing as she gargled blood. Just before the explosion tore through her body, separating her limbs and incinerating her brain, she had one final thought.
I'll live with it.

ABOUT THE AUTHOR

SPIKE BLACK writes fast-paced supernatural horror novels and high concept suspense thrillers. His obsessions include psychic phenomena, fate versus free will, and death. He's a laugh-a-minute at parties. He lives with his wife and two children in Suffolk, United Kingdom.

SPIKE BLACK'S
LEAVE THIS PLACE

Silas wakes with a start in the middle of the night, feeling a suffocating sense of unease - as if he's being watched. His wife is asleep. He scans the bedroom of their rented holiday cottage, a spooky and unfamiliar place.

He makes out something in the dark. On the chair in the corner of the room. *What the…?* He's mistaken, surely. It's his over-active imagination. It's a trick of the moonlight.

No. Something's there. A figure, hunched forward. An old man. The same old man he's seen in a framed photograph on the bedroom wall. Sitting there, watching them sleep. With a terrifying grin on his face…

Buy *Leave This Place* from Amazon

Made in the USA
San Bernardino, CA
12 December 2016